Strung Out

To

Die

A Divorced Diva

Mystery

Book One

Also by Tonya Kappes

Women's Fiction

Carpe Bead 'em

Anthologies

Something Spooky This Way Comes

Believe Christmas Anthology

Olivia Davis Paranormal Mystery Series

Splitsville.com

Color Me A Crime

Magical Cures Mystery Series

A Charming Crime

A Charming Cure

A Charming Potion

Grandberry Falls Series

The Ladybug Jinx

Happy New Life

A Superstitious Christmas

Never Tell Your Dreams

A Divorced Diva Beading Mystery Series

A Bead of Doubt Short Story

Strung Out To Die

Small Town Romance Short Story Series

A New Tradition

"Full of wit, humor and colorful characters, Tonya Kappes delivers a fun, fast-paced story that will leave you hooked!"

~Author of the Lifetime movie Flirty with Forty, Jane Porter

Dedications and Acknowledgments

I would like to thank my critique group, Heather Webber (Heather Blake), Shelley Shepard Grey, Hilda Knepp, and Cathy Liggett, for their endless love for the crazy Divorced Divas and supporting me through difficult writing times.

Hugs and kisses to my guys (Eddy, Jack, Austin, and Brady) for always being supportive. I love you guys!

Thank you Dru Ann Love, mystery reader extraordinaire, for taking time out of your busy schedule and beta read Strung Out to Die. Your insight is invaluable!

As always, my mom and dad for being my biggest cheerleaders. I can't imagine life without you!

Strung Out

To

Die

A Divorced Diva

Mystery

Book One

Chapter One

"She is going to be the death of me," I grumbled, wondering why Marlene had left the empty bead boxes stacked up next to the front door.

Wheak, wheak. Willow, my pet pig, trotted in and plopped down next to the stack of boxes. She was as good as a vacuum cleaner when it came to beads lying on the floor.

"No, Willow. No beads today, just empty boxes." I shooed her to the back as I slammed the front door with my foot.

The thin shop walls rattled, sending empty boxes tumbling to the floor. At least I thought they were empty until I heard glass beads trickling out onto the hardwood. Frantically, I pushed them out of the way and crawled on my hands and knees to stop the sparkly gems from rolling under the shelving unit that my stupid ex-husband had put up. Sean had a brilliant idea—or so he thought---that if he screwed the shelves up on the wall, it would make an excellent display, leaving a two-inch gap at the bottom.

Idiot.

I think he did it on purpose. He knows I hate to clean, especially under the beds, couches or anything that has an under. These shelves have just enough space underneath for the dust bunnies and loose beads to find a home.

"Ugh."

The Under.

Willow scrambled out of the back room, nose down and her tail twirling in the air as though she was about to take off ass first.

"Stop!" I yelled, throwing myself down on the ground. There was no way I was going to take her to the veterinarian for another enema. That was not a pretty sight for anyone involved. Especially a pig or the beautiful beads she so loved to gobble up.

Willow darted to the back, with her tail tucked as if she knew what would happen if she did eat another bead.

With my butt stuck up in the air, (which was not particularly my best attribute) I squeezed my eyes shut and shoved my hand into the depths of the unknown. I'm not very fond of putting my hand in *The Under*, much less a dark *Under*.

Head on the floor, I peeked into the dark abyss. I couldn't see a thing.

I stood up and adjusted my waistband. Yes, since my divorce from dumbass, I've gained a few extra pounds eating too many pieces of Agnes Pearl's homemade fudge. The spry eighty-five year-old wealthy widow pays Marlene in room, board, and fudge to take care of her. Because Marlene likes to stay the same size six, she brings the delightful chocolaty treats to me and the other Divorced Divas.

The Divas, for short, was a group formed in the most unlikely of ways. I was driving through Swanee on a rough day. Sean hadn't paid the alimony, and in the back of my head, I knew I needed to make a payment to the Sloan's for rent.

The church sign read, "If you are divorced. Stop here. Meeting at 7pm." As luck would have it, it was 7pm. I whipped my little VW Beetle into the parking lot and marched right in.

The women greeted me with open arms, and we've been close ever since.

We found laughter and tears while bashing our ex-husbands and cheering each other on. Diva Flora tended to take suggestions literally. Once, she cut all the armpits out of her husband's business shirts, put them in a garbage bag and dumped canned kidney beans on them. When he came to get his garbage bags of clothes, he had a little treat inside. Needless to say, the Divas group got a visit from Noah Druck, our local cop. He suggested we bash our ex-husbands, only figuratively from then on, unless we wanted a slew of lawsuits.

We Divas loved meeting and came up with all sorts of fun evil plots in our head, but that's where they stayed. The church wasn't able to accommodate additional meeting times, so we moved them to different Diva's houses and then finally to The Beaded Dragonfly.

I glanced around again, looking at the unswept floor and all the bead boards lying on the table that still had wire clippings and crimp beads that needed to go in the trash. Obviously, Marlene hadn't gotten around to any of the closing cleanup, which surprised me since I saw her in the parking lot of The Livin' End bar when I was leaving.

After work last night, I went to grab a quick drink at the bar with my best friend Ginger Sloan Rush. I left Marlene to finish the nightly chores, which included checking off the new inventory, cleaning the bead boards, and taking out the trash. She hadn't said a word about not finishing her work at the shop. She'd just been eager to get into the bar.

There wasn't anything worse than coming in on a Saturday morning, The Beaded Dragonfly's busiest day, to a room full of mostly empty boxes with a few stray beads left in them, before I'd even had my second cup of coffee; especially when I had my very first bride coming in for her consultation.

The bride, Margaret McGee, was the break I needed. This job was exactly what I needed to help get me back into the black. If I could land this client, I was sure she had several bride-to-be friends, and they might also need some jewelry. I rubbed my hands together hoping this was my break.

I was tired of depending on Sean's alimony along with a few beading customers here and there to make ends meet.

I looked back at the boxes. *Of all days.*

I pay Marlene to do those things. It was only minimum wage, but at least it's better than nothing. Plus, she got to design and make all the jewelry she wanted—for free. That was exactly what she wanted when she first stepped her high-heeled shoes into The Beaded Dragonfly.

I rummaged through the desk drawer to see if I could find a flashlight so I could track down the runaway beads.

I got sidetracked when someone tapped on the door and looked up. I had only thirty minutes until the shop opened, and I needed all thirty to get at least some of the out-of-stock items filled. I'd have to trust that Beautiful Beads Wholesale sent everything I ordered.

There stood Noah Druck with his hand on his holster like he was ready for some gun slinging right there on the steps of my bead shop.

The beads lost to *The Under* were going to have to wait.

Noah folded his massive arms across his chest as he waited for me to unlock the door. Lines creased between his brows as he narrowed them.

If he wasn't a cop, I might be interested. He'd come around a time or two to the cottage to make sure no one was bothering me, and on both occasions we had a beer and a little friendly banter, but nothing came of it.

His compelling blue eyes, firm features, and confident shoulders told me he was here on more than just a friendly visit.

"Morning, Holly." Noah took his hat off, leaving a ring around his dark hair.

I felt the urge to ruffle it up a bit, like I did my carpet when something like my laundry basket sat in one spot for too long, but resisted.

"Well what brings you over to The Beaded Dragonfly this morning? A glass bead bracelet to go with your police blues?" I referred to his uniform, and wanted to lighten the tension I found forming around his eyes.

He shuffled his body weight to each side and moved his hand back down to rest on his gun. There it was. The flashlight I needed was neatly attached to his holster. I felt my eyes light up like a starry night.

"Can I come in?"

Without even answering or waiting for an answer, he pushed by me into the shop. I backed up to oblige, keeping my eye on the prize.

I reached out in hopes I could just borrow the flashlight for just a couple minutes, only for him to smack my hand away.

"What are you doing?" His eyes narrowed suspiciously. "Just because I've known you all my life, doesn't give you the right to grab things from me while I'm on duty."

I pulled back, realizing he was right. He was never too far behind Sean when we were in high school. It was as if I was the third wheel. Once we got married, Sean and Noah had a falling out, leaving just the two of us in the marriage.

"I need a flashlight for a second." I pointed to it.

With a finger flick, he had it out of the holster, flipped it in the air, and handed it to me.

"All you have to do is ask and maybe bat a couple eyelashes."

I did my best batting and took it.

"Where's Marlene?" His posture straightened up and his neck craned to see in the back of the shop.

"Don't get me started on her. Hold onto this for a second." I gave him the flashlight back.

I'd forgotten about the boxes I needed to get out of the way before any customers came in. *The Under* was going to have to wait some more. I stacked a couple of the boxes on top of each other.

"I really need to talk to her." He put the flashlight on one of the bead tables. "Let me help you with those."

"No. I've got it." There was no way I was going to let him see the messy storage room. "What do you want to talk to her about?"

A twinge of jealousy found a pit in my stomach. Men were always falling all over Marlene. He definitely didn't fit her main requirements. Rich. Rich. RICH.

"Doug Sloan didn't make it home last night from The Livin' End." He stacked another box on top of the ones already in my arms, making the load a little heavy since it was filled with beads. "And as a favor to the Sloan's, I said I'd look into it."

I peered around the armful of cardboard and laughed.

It wasn't unusual for Doug to flaunt the Sloan name around and watch women lay down at his feet. He'd probably hooked up with a young floozy who knew better than to let him go home last night. Marlene would be crushed since she'd been trying to get her claws into Mr. Moneybags for months.

Doug was my best friend and Ginger's younger brother. The Sloan's owned almost everything in Swanee, including the cottage I was living in. They owned the hardware shop, the bank, and the grocery store.

The only things they didn't own were small businesses like The Beaded Dragonfly and Sean's carpentry business, aptly named Sean's Little Shack. I never said he was smart, just good in bed.

"You know Doug; he probably went home with some girl." I hollered over my shoulder on my way back to the storage room. "That will break Marlene's…"

Something on the floor caused me lose my footing. I teetered and tottered, trying to steady the boxes, but it was too late. The boxes tumbled to the floor, and the beads bounced all over and into The Under. Willow darted out like a vacuum, snorting up all the beads she could.

"Damn." Disappointed, I turned back toward the storage room door to see what the hell Marlene had left laying on the floor. I let out a blood curdling scream. "Oh my, God!"

It was Doug Sloan.

"What?" Noah ran back as fast as he could. He drew his gun. "Step back, Holly. And take this pig with you."

I tried to wrangle the bead-eating pet, but she continued to squeal and run the other way when I'd reach for her.

"Holly, please." Noah looked back and begged as Willow took something near Doug's head and ran off. "Get that out of her mouth!"

"Here, Willow." I called for her.

She ran in circles around the table, making me lose my footing again and I fell on my butt.

"Ouch!"

Some beads that were on the floor got embedded in the palm of my hand where I tried to catch my fall.

"Get her!" Noah was still trying to protect Doug—and the crime scene—from Willow's interference.

Willow squealed her way toward him. Her tail was twirling around like one of those beanie hats with the propeller on top.

"Pull her tail! She'll spit it out!" I screamed reaching out.

I immediately jumped up and ran over to try to get whatever it was out of her snout. The last thing I wanted her eating was any part of Doug Sloan.

"Pull her tail?" Noah's eyes had a fear in them I'd never seen.

"You aren't scared of a pig, are you?" I pulled Willow's tail and out popped a few of the black and white swirl cat eye beads.

Whew! I was never so happy to see cat eye beads. I was sure she had picked up a body part.

"No. I'm scared because Doug Sloan is dead." Noah picked up the beads before Willow could suck them up again and held them out in the palm of his hand. "And the weapon looks like it was a string of these. Willow's eating my evidence."

Chapter Two

The police tape wrapped all the way around the shop caused a flurry of activity outside. The police didn't let anyone in, or me out. Thank God, Willow used kitty litter, or we'd have been in trouble.

"Let's go over this one more time." Noah had me sitting in a chair at one of the bead tables while he read through his notes. "You left Marlene here and went to go meet Ginger at The Livin' End."

Slowly I nodded.

"But Ginger didn't show up, right?" He repeated my statement with a question.

"Right," I agreed.

"You saw Sean and Doug at The Livin' end." Noah looked like he was in the third grade, using his pencil to track what he had written from the questions he had asked me earlier.

"Were they talking to each other?" He looked up from under his eyebrows.

"Umm, hmm." My lips pinched together. I wasn't going to let anything slip out of them.

I rolled a bead between my pincer finger and thumb as I thought about the conversation—make that the fight I overheard---between Sean and Doug at The Livin' End last night. But there was no way I was going to give up any more information than I needed to.

Had Sean killed Doug? I wondered, gazing back at Dead Doug's spot. *And if he did, why? Why here? Why frame me?*

I couldn't wait to get my hands on Sean Harper.

Leaning to the right, I zeroed in on Noah's little notepad. He was writing way more information down than I had relayed to him.

Don't change your posture. I repeated in my head. I had seen far too many CSI TV shows to know that when a police officer questions you, they were taking in everything from the way the suspect sits, to the way they play with their fingers. . . *Wait! Am I a suspect?*

His eyes narrowed, and he jerked the pad closer to his chest. "And you *didn't* come back here after Ginger failed to show up? And you didn't know Doug was coming here?"

"No, and no, to both questions." My heartbeat quickened and I folded my hands in my lap so he couldn't see them shaking.

Suddenly, I was feeling like a suspect, when all I did was literally stumble across Doug's dead body.

One of the officers slid across the floor, thanks to the entire bead debacle and with a flurry of expletives, he fell and ended up feet-first in *The Under* with the beads he slipped on. I watched them roll to The Under, secretly wishing I were down there, too.

In the back of the shop, the phone was ringing off the hook. Thank God, I didn't have a cell phone. I knew the Divas must have been desperately trying to get in touch with me.

"Free Holly!"

There was a small group of people gathered outside of the shop, chanting with their fists pumping in the air. Agnes Pearl stood in front of the group leading them. I couldn't help but smile at the spry eighty-five year-old.

A police officer stood in front of them with his hands out, barring them from coming up the steps.

The phone continued to ring. Normally I hate talking on the phone, but right now, it would be better than sitting here under the interrogation of Noah Druck.

"Can I get that?" I asked him.

"Fine, answer it."

I jumped up before he could change his mind. If I was lucky, I might slip and fall from the loose beads on the floor and knock myself out.

"And don't say a word about the murder to anyone," he chirped over his shoulder.

"The Beaded Dragonfly," I answered as upbeat as I could, I was sure it was Flora calling from outside, but it wasn't.

"What on earth is going on over there?" Bernadine Frisk, one of the Divorced Divas asked.

I could practically feel her beady, jade eyes searing the phone line. "I heard that the police have you surrounded!"

"Free Holly!" Agnes had both fists in the air now, and a scowl on her face.

I swallowed hard, looking around. There seemed to be a lot of police officers' eyes focused on me. "I. . ." I couldn't think straight. It was as if the police officers wanted to hear what I was going to say.

Suddenly, my mouth dried. My eyes darted between all of the policemen staring at me. Unabashedly eavesdropping, they had stopped dusting the beads, chair legs, tables, and doorknobs. *Did they think that I killed Doug?*

"Holly?" Patience wasn't one of Diva Bernadine's best traits. "What's going on? I heard Doug Sloan was found in there. Dead. Is that true?"

"Well, yes. But I'm not allowed to say anything." Cautiously choosing my words, I added, "Yet."

"Does this mean we aren't going to be able to meet there tonight?" Bernadine asked, as if a dead Doug Sloan wasn't reason enough to postpone a Diva's meeting.

"I haven't had time to think about it. Hold on." I covered the mouth of the phone and said to Noah, "When am I getting my shop back?"

"Not tonight." Noah looked at the other officers and motioned for them to get back to work. He brushed fingerprint dust on anything clean.

"Not tonight, Bernadine." I wondered how long I was going to have to stay. I wondered if I needed a lawyer, but was too afraid to ask. If I asked, it would seem as if I was guilty, if I didn't, it still seemed like I was guilty. So I just kept my mouth shut. "Can you call all the other Divas and tell them we need to reschedule for tomorrow night?"

"Yes I will, but I will be. . ." I didn't let her finish her sentence. I was in a full-crisis situation, and meeting with the Divas wasn't on the top of my priority list.

Besides, I knew she'd be waiting on my steps when I got home. After all, she only lived across the lake. Bernadine was the Diva who had to know everything going on in Swanee, especially something big like this.

I hung up the phone and noticed white dust all over the cradle, then realized the powdery mix now covered every surface, and my beautiful beads were no longer glistening. My head hurt thinking about cleaning each and every bead by hand. And how much of an investment I had in them, only to possibly be going to jail for a murder I did not commit.

I couldn't go to jail, and I had a huge balance on my credit card to pay off.

A police officer with a broom was sweeping up the beads per Noah's orders.

"Hey!" I yelled. The police officer looked at me. "Do you think you could clean under those shelves?"

After a moment's pause, he shrugged and bent down, sweeping the broom through the two-inch *Under*. Beads and dust went everywhere. The officer waved his hand to clear the plume of dust around his head.

Pretty darn pleased that I didn't have to clean it, I glanced over at Noah, who was giving me the stink-eye. I needed to make a quick phone call.

"I have a client consultation this morning. I think I should call and reschedule." I really hated to call the McGee's, but I'm sure they had already heard from the Sloans.

"Fine." Noah gestured to me to go ahead. "Hurry up. And don't say anything about Doug."

Margaret McGee didn't answer at the cell phone number she'd left on The Beaded Dragonfly's answering machine. Unfortunately, it was the only number I had for her. I really hoped she checked her messages and wouldn't just show up and see this mess, because if she did, she probably wouldn't let me design and make the accessories for her bridal party. That wouldn't be good.

I was counting on her giving me referrals since she was Swanee's reigning beauty queen and president of The

Junior League. Plus she was the daughter of Swanee's city attorney, Bear McGee.

Margaret McGee knew a lot of people who I was sure could use a beaded jewelry maker like me.

Chapter Three

Once the police were finished and Doug was removed from my storeroom floor, I took a minute for myself. Normally, I'd walk Willow to help clear my head, but not today. Especially not on the Main Street of Swanee. Everyone was still milling around the shop, anxious for news.

Noah's words rang loud and clear in my mind. "Holly, we really need to get a statement about exactly what you were doing last night. If you don't cooperate, I'll be forced to bring you in for formal questioning."

I couldn't shake the notion that I might not only be a key witness, but Noah seemed to be alluding that I might be a suspect along with Sean. I walked back to the boxes where I found Willow lying in one of them. Her little dark-spotted pink body was almost too cute to wake up, but I had to get these boxes out of the way, and moving them helped to clear my mind.

Could Sean really have killed him?

"I'll get you back for this," was all I could recall overhearing Sean say to Doug last night when I was leaving The Livin' End.

Fear knotted in my belly. Had I really been married to a killer?

No. No way! Sure, Sean was a jerk and would purposely leave the toilet seat up at night because he knew darn good and well that I pee every single night at two a.m., and leaving up the seat would cause me to fall in, but there was no way he was capable of murder.

If he was, why Doug?

Doug Sloan's work wasn't as good as Sean's was, and he did get most of the carpentry jobs for the city and private residences, but that was only because he had the last name of Sloan. Even then, Sean would go behind and clean up fifty-percent of Doug's messes. Being the good friend I am, I had never let it come between Ginger, and me, even when I was married to Sean.

I flinched when I heard a knock on the door. Willow jumped up, wide-awake, and ran back to the storage closet as fast as her little hooves would carry her.

I had just gotten rid of the police. The last thing I wanted was a nosy visitor trying to check out Doug's chalk outline.

I shoved the boxes into the furthest corner to get them out of the way. These beads were not going to get put out today. I'd be cleaning all the dust the police left behind.

Turning the corner, I was surprised to see Diva Marlene's hot-pink nails tearing the police tape in half. When she saw me coming, she smiled, waving me over to unlock the door.

Reluctantly, I did.

Marlene wasted no time getting to the heart of the matter.

"What happened to Doug? Did the police name a suspect?" Marlene chomped her gum and pushed her way into The Beaded Dragonfly.

Willow ran back out to see who was making all the commotion.

I'd never seen someone chew the hell out of a piece of gum like Marlene did, one piece after another. Many times, I'd had to remind her not to chew so loud during beading class, because no one else could concentrate.

"That pig is going to be a 'pig on a stick' if my high-heels catch her one day." Marlene smacked her lips together and chased Willow back into the storage room.

Groink, groink, groink, Willow snorted out of sight.

Marlene loved to dress in leopard print *anything,* including high-heels. I'm not sure what her deceased husband did when he was alive, but he sure kept her looking good. Even on her days off, she wore heels. "You never know who you're going to run into," she always said, with her acrylic nails batting the air. Amazingly, those claws didn't stop her from beading.

"That's not nice, Marlene. Willow will get you back one day." I picked up the feather duster and lightly brushed it across the hanging strings of beads on the shelves.

Marlene and Willow had a history. Once, when she first come to town, she wanted me to wrap her fancy yellow Spinel diamond so she could hang it from a necklace. Unfortunately, Willow, who will eat anything, snacked on Marlene's precious stone. Doc Johnson's x-ray of my sick piggy confirmed that she had eaten the gem.

After Willow passed the gem, (and by that I mean she pooped it out) Marlene took it back and decided she was going to learn the wrapping technique herself, which was fine by me. She and Willow had been at odds ever since.

Marlene threw her hot-pink hobo bag on the counter and pointed at the dust all over the place. "Fingerprint dust?"

"Yep, Noah wasn't worried about skimping on the powder." Shaking my head back and forth, I began thinking I should just grab all the beads and dunk them in soapy water. "I'm sorry about Doug."

"I don't know what is going on with my love life!" With her elbows firmly planted on the dusty countertop, she rested her head in her hands.

Condolences seemed to be in order since she had just landed Doug after chasing him the past few months.

"Every time I think I find 'The One', they up and die on me." Sighing, she picked up the polishing rag to help clean the sterling silver beads. "I thought I had a chance with him, too." She raised her shoulders, craned her neck to look over at the tape outline of Doug Sloan's body.

I'm assuming she was talking about Doug, not Sean. There was no sense in trying to be Veronica Mars when I was sure Sean wasn't the killer. He might be a snake, but he wasn't a python.

I put it in the back of my head and dusted the beading tools—even those hadn't been safe from Noah's powder.

Setting the rag back on the counter, Marlene dug in her purse and pulled out another stick of gum. "Want one?" She shoved the pack in my face.

"No, thanks," I mumbled. I couldn't chew gum, clean the shop, and try to solve this murder. Multi-tasking wasn't one of my fortes.

"Agnes said Noah Druck came by and asked her all sorts of questions about the work Doug had done for her." She chomped.

It was no secret that Sean was contracted by Agnes to go in and clean up Doug's shoddy job. Agnes had made sure she told everyone about it. She even went as far as putting a big sign in her yard the size of a football scoreboard. It had blinking lights and all and said, *Doug Sloan=BAD BUSINESS!*

Lawyer, Bear McGee, paid a visit to Agnes and threatened a lawsuit on Doug's behalf if she didn't take it down. She threatened one back, and included a death threat in her response. Foolish woman was probably regretting those words now.

"I told her to keep her mouth shut. A little old woman like Agnes couldn't hurt a flea." Marlene picked up a handful of beads and wiped them half-heartedly. "You think Sean did it?"

I did a double take. I swear there was a glint in her eye.

"Why would you say that?" I grabbed the window cleaner and sprayed it on the counter top.

"Well. . .Doug *was* killed in *your* shop, Holly." She unrolled one too many paper towels.

I grabbed the roll from her. If she was right, my alimony would stop and I'd need to be conservative with everything, including paper towels. Marlene wasn't good at conserving anything, including men.

"That doesn't mean Sean did it." My brows furrowed. Why did I feel the need to defend him when he could be setting me up?

"Think about it." There was a bubble pop between her breaths. "He has to pay you alimony. Doug was found in your shop. I even heard a string of beads was found around his neck."

Bad news traveled fast. Especially around Swanee.

I swear my heart stopped. What if it wasn't about bad blood between Sean and Doug? What if it was about me and the alimony payments?

"If you're convicted and put in jail, Sean doesn't have to pay you a dime. Men can be weasels, honey. Especially when it comes to money."

Nervously, I scrubbed the countertop wondering if Sean had really set me up. But he didn't do a good job if he was publicly arguing with Doug at The Livin' End.

"I was there, you know. At the Livin' End last night. I saw Sean threaten him," she confirmed. "The note said to meet Doug at The Livin' End, and when I went there he acted like he never sent it." She rolled her eyes just before a big bubble popped on her face. "That's when Sean confronted him about Agnes and how he was sick and tired of Doug taking advantage of all the elderly folks in town. Between me and you, he even said that someone needed to stop Doug Sloan."

I didn't say anything. I had to talk to Sean and get a firsthand account. But one question hadn't been answered. Why was Doug dead in my shop?

"Marlene, weren't you supposed meet him here last night?" I had to throw it out there. Let's face it. Marlene blew into Swanee without telling us much about her past. Somehow, she had talked Agnes, our octogenarian Diva friend, into hiring her as her caregiver without showing any credentials. Agnes might be a couple cups of crazy, but she always knew where her money was. I couldn't imagine someone putting one over on Agnes.

Marlene's eyes narrowed and her mouth pursed. "Holly Harper, are you accusing me of killing Doug Sloan?"

"Just asking." I put my hands up in front of me in case her nails felt the need to claw something. "He was found dead in my business, and it wasn't a secret you've been trying to land him since the day you laid your cosmetically implanted lashes on him."

I'm not sure how old Marlene was, and couldn't guess. Everything she had was enhanced, and not by God himself.

I took a closer look at those eyelashes. I'd never heard of anything like it until she told the Divas about her eyelash implant surgery and the money she spent on it.

"I'll admit he was a challenge, but I'd never kill for a man to love me. What sense does that make? I need him alive! I'm going home. I have a headache. Let me know when the next Diva meeting is." She tossed her pink bag over her shoulder and slammed the door behind her.

It was probably all the gum chomping that was rattling her brain making it hurt, but she was good at leaving when a situation became sticky. Like the first time she met Ginger Sloan Rush, my best friend and Doug's older sister. Ginger could spot a phony in a second, and it was clear she had her doubts about Marlene and had practically given her a grand inquisition.

If it weren't for Ginger, the Divas would've never known Marlene was a wealthy widow, even though she never told us how her previous husband died. When we asked, her lips pinched tighter than bark on a tree.

I looked out the window and watched Marlene strut down Main Street toward Agnes Pearl's house, which happened to be right next to Ginger's house. Agnes Pearl was going to get a visit from me very soon.

But first, there were a couple of phone calls I needed to make. I dialed.

"Bernadine, it's me." I glanced around to make sure no one was listening, even though I knew there wasn't anyone in the shop. Obviously I couldn't be too careful now-a-days. I cupped my hand over the handset and spoke softly, "Be at my house in fifteen minutes. Emergency meeting. Call the Divas."

Without a word, Bernadine knew exactly what I meant. I hung up the phone.

"Come on, girl." I yelled for Willow. When she came waddling in the shop from the back, I bent down and clipped her leash to her collar. I glanced around at what was once a sparkly, shiny bead shop, and frowned.

One thing I was sure of, Doug Sloan was found dead in my shop and no one was coming forward to admit to killing him. I had a sneaky suspicion that I was being set up, but by whom?

It was going to be up to the Divas and me to find out.

Chapter Four

Jim Rush's truck was backed up to the barn behind my house when I got home. It wasn't unusual for him to be there about that time, but it seemed a little odd today, considering Doug's murder. Then again, Ginger and Jim owned the property and the cottage that I was living in. They used the barn to store extra equipment for Sloan's Hardware, another company Ginger's family owned in Swanee, and Jim was the manager.

I craned my neck to see inside the open barn door. I'd never been inside since it was off limits. Jim had made that crystal clear with the handshake agreement we made about the living arrangements. A handshake was taken just as seriously as a written contract in Swanee. Besides, Ginger and I were best friends. If you can't trust your best friend or her husband, whom can you trust?

Then again, I was beginning to wonder about the answer to that question.

"Hi, Holly." Jim and his ten-gallon cowboy hat appeared out of nowhere in the barn doorway. His eyes were red around the lids. He took his hat off and whacked it up against his legs. Dirt came flying out of it. "I had to get away."

A cloud of dust following him as he shuffled closer.

Jim always wore his jeans all the way up to his navel. These jeans weren't just any blue, either. They were the bluest blue you've ever seen; indigo in fact. His big money-sign belt buckle was always polished and front and center, keeping his neatly pressed collared shirt tucked in tight.

The color of the shirt changed daily, but you could bet he'd always be in an identical pair of blue jeans, with the same belt buckle and cowboy boots day in and day out.

But not today.

His slicked back, coal black hair flopped to the side. And his shirt was wrinkled and untucked, and those jeans of his were a little on the gray side.

"I'm sorry about Doug." I wasn't sure what to say, since he was found dead in my shop. "I don't know why he was at The Beaded Dragonfly."

I did wonder if Ginger suspected I had something to do with Doug's murder and hoped Jim would say something---anything---to make me feel better.

"Do you have anything you want to tell me, Holly?" he asked, staring at me in a peculiar, almost accusing way. "Ginger and I can't figure out why he'd be there either."

"I have no clue." I shook my head. It was a question I'd asked myself over and over again the past few hours. The sick feeling had now settled to scared stiff. Obviously, they considered me a suspect. But why? What would my motive for strangling Doug Sloan be? Clearing my throat, I asked, "How is Ginger?"

"Distraught." Sadness was all over his face. "Ginger and I want answers."

He turned to go back to the barn, but stopped. "I wish you would've installed those cameras," he muttered as he walked back to shut the barn door and then jumped into his truck.

He hadn't made me feel better at all.

As I watched him drive away, I wished he'd talked me into those security cameras too.

When I first opened The Beaded Dragonfly, Jim's security business, Rush's Protective Services, was flourishing. He'd even offered me a deal.

"I'll give you three cameras for the price of two." I recalled him holding up the cameras that were no bigger than the palm of my hand, but the price tag was huge.

Eight thousand dollars was just more than I had to invest.

"I can't afford my own house, much less eight thousand dollars worth of camera equipment." I'd reminded him of our handshake agreement.

"What about the alimony money?" he'd asked.

"What alimony?" I laughed. "Doug gets all the jobs around here."

That was the end of that conversation. Eight thousand dollars sounded like a great investment now.

I turned around and looked at the gray clapboard, three-room cottage I called home. It was all I needed after my divorce. Three rooms were big enough for all the stuff I had collected over the years. The best part wasn't the wall of windows that overlooked the lake or the fact that Ginger pays someone to squeegee them, but the furniture.

It came fully furnished and the only '*Unders*' in the entire place were beneath the futon and the claw-foot tub.

The cabinets in the kitchen went all the way down to the floor. There wasn't a kitchen table to worry about sweeping under, no book shelves to dust under, no *Unders* whatsoever.

There were built-in bookshelves in the family room. The bedroom was plain and simple with just a box spring and mattress. The closet was all I needed for what little clothes I was fitting into at the time.

I stopped shy of the door after I heard a rustling sound behind me. I bolted upright, and stiffened, trying not to move, blink, or even breathe.

Was the real killer already here to claim my life?

Willow sniffed the paver stones. My nerves were getting the best of me. Someone might be out there to get me, but they'd be stupid to try in the daylight?

"Psst," someone said from the shaking bushes.

I jumped. Putting my hands up in the only karate chop position I knew, I scream, "Watch out, I'm armed and dangerous!"

"With what? That pig?" The whisper that was loud but familiar, gave way to laughter. The bush shook again. "Holly, look over here."

I looked. The pink sneakers sticking out from the bushes were a dead give-away.

"Bernadine, what are you doing in there?" I parted the twigs, but Willow had already begun her ritual of licking Bernadine.

"Ouch!" Bernadine untangled her long crimson hair that was caught up in the bush and pushed Willow away. "I didn't want Jim to see me since it was his brother-in-law that was killed in the shop. Enough, Willow."

Willow liked Bernadine. Well, she liked the cut up apples and grapes that Bernadine kept in a Ziploc baggie in her pocket.

"Food Watchers," she would claim, holding the snack up every time I suggested she keep them at home. As long as I've known Bernadine, she'd been on Food Watchers. Only she really didn't watch her food or her weight. She'd always been the same five-foot-one and a little on the plump side.

The keys jingled and jangled as I tried to pry the door open. With a swift kick to the bottom corner and a little nudge, the door opened. Willow flew in, anticipating a spot on the futon right next to Bernadine and her Ziploc baggie.

"I really need to get that fixed," I said, referring to the door as I threw the keys in the basket on the counter top.

Bernadine walked in behind me, nearly knocking me out of the way. The keys fell to the ground. She hung them up on the hook and straightened the remaining items in the basket. I'd gotten used to it. She was a neat freak. "There is a rightful place for everything," she said.

Yes, there was, and a Dead Doug's rightful place was not on the floor of my bead shop.

"Did you call Ginger?"

Bernadine grabbed a carrot stick out of her Ziploc, breaking the silence with a big crunch. "No." She chomped, looking at me as if I had two heads. "Do you honestly think she feels like coming to an emergency meeting? Especially since it has to do with her dead brother lying on the floor of *your* shop."

"Yeah, you're right." Although I hadn't called Ginger, and knew that she wasn't terribly fond of Doug and his sneaky ways, I was sure she didn't want to see him dead. She was my best friend and couldn't think that I actually killed him. *Could she?*

Bernadine chased her carrot stick with a few pea pods. I cringed at the thought of eating a pea pod and the reality of calling Ginger.

The door flew open and Willow nearly broke her legs running to the back of the cottage out of shear flight.

"What's the emergency?" Diva Flora bolted in the door with her designer bag hanging off the crook of one arm, and a stack of glass-beaded bracelets jingling on the other. Her cell phone was pressed up to her ear, as usual. "No, not you. I'll call you back. And don't think you are getting my Cher albums!" She flipped her phone shut and threw it in her bag.

Out of all the Divas, Flora never missed a bead class or an opportunity to make a beaded bracelet.

This was a first. I glanced at the space between her shoulder and ear. I looked for a charging station in that space because Flora was rarely seen without her phone planted there.

"Who died?" She glanced at her outstretched hand inspecting her nails.

"Doug Sloan," I muttered. She obviously hadn't heard about the murder, which wasn't unusual because she was probably on the phone all day.

Flora's mouth formed an 'O.' "You mean Ginger's Doug Sloan?" Nervously she ran her hands through her thick wavy brown hair and pulled it back into a makeshift ponytail. The color seemed to fade from her high-cheek bones, leaving her a little gaunt, making her look her actual age of fifty.

Slowly, Bernadine and I nodded. Slower, she eased herself on the couch next to us.

Quietly, she added, "So, this is what the meeting is about."

We nodded. . .again.

"How? Spill it." She reached in her bag and grabbed the vibrating phone. Even in an emergency, she still couldn't leave the phone alone. A good reason I didn't have a cell. I didn't want to be tied to it. "I'll call you back!" she chirped, and then flipped it shut. "It was only Benni," she explained, "Again."

It was like her ex's name was attached to her eyeballs. Every time she said his name, her eyes rolled.

"We are actually fighting over who gets the record album collection." She shrugged her shoulders. "I'll be damned if I let him and what's-his-name drink wine to *my* Cher albums."

Her divorce was a messy one. They had been married for twenty years when he came out and told her he was gay. "I'll make that bastard pay," she'd say. She didn't mind telling people how much she got in alimony. Needless to say, it was four times what I got. I guess lawyers really do make a lot more than carpenters do.

Now, even though her divorce was final, they still hadn't split all the property. She put her distaste for him aside when I needed the papers filed for the shop. He'd done them free. Flora claimed he still owed her. I wondered if he'd ever done a murder case.

"Holly, are you okay?" Flora asked.

I nodded. Not really, but who would be if someone were in my shoes. Everyone needed to hurry up. There wasn't any sticky situation that we Divas haven't figured out; only those situations didn't involve murder.

The knock at the door made us all jump. I guess we were all on edge.

Cheri stood on the other side when I opened the door. She was as cute as ever with her plaid beret perched on top of her head.

She was a college student that rented the one bedroom apartment above the shop. She was rarely home because she spent most her time on campus studying. She did keep an eye on the shop for me every now-and-then, or took Willow on quick walks.

"I got her message, but I had already heard the news. Thank God I was at the library pulling an all-nighter." She took the beret off her head and used her fingers to re-spike her hair as she walked in and planted herself in a chair. "It's all over campus that there's a killer on the loose."

"Carrot?" Bernadine leaned over offering a snack from the bag. Cheri took a carrot stick.

The crackle from the plastic sent Willow flying down the hall and she planted her butt in front of Cheri, who was a sucker for Willow's little beady eyes. Cheri fed Willow the carrot. Once in her mouth, Willow darted back down the hall with her tail twirling in the air.

"Wait." Flora put her hand in the air. "What exactly happened?"

I stood in front of my friends. It was now time to put all our real sleuthing that we used on our ex-husbands to the test. I cleared my throat.

"Doug was found dead on the floor of the Beaded Dragonfly with a strand of black cat eye beads around his neck." I put my hand to my chest. "I did not kill him, but someone wants the police to think I did."

Flora picked at the cat eye bracelet on her arm.

"Marlene believes that Sean is the murderer, and for good reasons. I will deal with Sean," I added.

"Where is that gold-digger, Marlene?" Flora glanced around. "She is an honorary Diva."

"I didn't call her, nor Agnes, or Ginger." Bernadine glanced around at the other Divas. "We are the original Diva's and I felt this was a matter for just us."

"I called this meeting because I need your help more than ever." It was time to put our big talkin' ways to the test. "I need y'all to help me figure out who is framing me and why."

"I'm in." Bernadine's eyes were big as she bit down on another carrot stick.

"Me too, girl." Flora slowly nodded, her eyes narrowed as if she was already formulating a plan in her head.

"For sure!" Cheri rubbed her hands together.

Now that I had their support, it was time to give out jobs.

"Okay, Cheri. Last night Sean and Doug had a fight at The Livin' End. Can you go down there and get the bar tender and regulars talking about it. This shouldn't be hard since Doug is the talk of the town."

"I can." She pulled her beret over her hair and headed out the door.

"Flora, can you get Bennie's private investigator to take a look around the Beaded Dragonfly? Inside and out. There was no visible cause of a break-in, so there has to be something somewhere." I know this was a tall request; after all, the private investigator followed her for months, never once leaving her alone.

Before I said another word, Flora was already on her cell and walking out. "Babbs, it's Flora Branson. I need to talk to that no-good boss of yours, now!"

The door slammed behind her.

"What can I do?" Bernadine's face lit up with excitement.

"You can help me lose weight." I crossed my arms in front of me. "I'm going to need to be in fighting shape when I kick this killer's ass."

I peered out the window, and over the lake. Someone was out to frame me and I wasn't going to sit around and let it happen. I was going to find them; somewhere, somehow.

Chapter Five

Groink, groink. Willow ran to the door when she heard a knock.

I didn't get an ounce of shuteye. And I wasn't expecting anyone this early. Pulling the covers up over my head, I tried to ignore the loud knocking and the loud voice in my heading telling me that it was probably the police coming to arrest me.

Flinging the covers off my body, I jumped up when I realized I hadn't done a damn thing to help my cause. Sure, I divvied out a few orders to the Divas.

If the police were here to take me in, they were going to have to take me kicking and screaming.

My foot knocked the old rotary phone that was lying on the floor off the hook. Willow had a habit of knocking it off the bedside table when she scrambled under the bed.

Seeing the phone made me feel a little better. Maybe someone had been trying to call me and couldn't get through. Maybe it was Noah telling me that the police had found the killer and I was off the hook. Better yet, maybe Sean was in jail. Well, I really didn't *want* Sean to be the killer.

I owed rent on the Beaded Dragonfly, so I needed the alimony. If Sean were in jail, I wouldn't get the alimony and be able to pay the rent.

Damn. I let out a sigh, pulling on my big yellow bath robe.

Bam, bam, bam.

"I'm coming!" I yelled, when the knock grew louder. I took my time picking up the phone and putting it back in its rightful place.

To my pleasant surprise, Bernadine stood on the other side of the door, with her pink tennis shoes and jogging suit on and yet another Ziploc baggie full of veggies in hand.

"Morning, Holly. I was taking a walk and thought you might want to join me. I called your phone but it rang busy." She jogged into the house, and then moseyed over to the futon. She put the veggies in her pocket and ran her hand along the crumpled up quilt. She folded it, neatly placing it back over the arm. "I would've called your cell. Oh, wait. You don't have one."

There's no reason for me to have a cell phone. I'm only responsible for one person and that would be me. I'm with me all the time; therefore, I have no reason to call myself. I'm always at home or at the shop, and both places have phones.

"Good thing you live just across the lake so you could just stop by," I said with a hint of sarcasm and pointed across the lake to her much larger log cabin.

She was here for one reason and one reason only—to get me in fighting shape.

Bernadine was right; I did need to exercise, not just to control my weight, but also to help me deal with the stress of finding Doug Sloan's dead rump on my bead shop floor.

She looked at me squarely.

"Fine!" I walked back to the bedroom and pulled out the only jogging suit I had. I held it up. My nose curled. Orange was not my favorite choice to wear, and a jumpsuit didn't look good on plump girls.

"Come on." Bernadine yelled from the other room. "Did you forget we have a killer to find?"

I shuffled to the bathroom to splash a little water on my face in hopes it would help me wake up. The white-tiled bathroom was perfect for my minimalist decorating style.

I looked in the mirror, noticing the black circles that had found a home under my tired eyes. "I bet jail has gray walls. Not a good color for me", I told the image staring back at me.

There was little to no motivation in me. With a heavy sigh, I turned on the water, and used my hands to throw it all over my face.

Every time I closed my eyes, I saw Doug lying on the storage room floor with that strand of cat eye beads around his neck. A few more splashes still couldn't wash away the image.

"I think Willow is hungry. She's trying to eat my bracelet." I detected a hint of irritation in Bernadine's voice.

I walked back down the short hallway, lined with pictures of generations of Sloans. From what I understood, they used the cottage as getaway on the weekends.

Ginger had told me to make it my home until I could afford a down payment on my own, but it felt funny changing out the human pictures for piggy photos.

"Come on, girly." I patted my leg for Willow to follow me to the refrigerator.

Willow hopped off the futon, nudged her ball, and trotted over. I've never understood the affection she has for all things round. Peas, balls, beads, and Bernadine.

I took a leftover ear of corn from the other night's dinner and handed it to her like she was a child. Eagerly, she took it and lay in the dog bed happily chomping away. I'd purchased the bed thinking she would use it to sleep in. Not a chance. She sleeps snuggled right up against me; hot piggy belly and all.

"Are you ready?" I couldn't believe those words were coming out of my mouth. Nor did I believe that I was having Bernadine get me in fighting shape. "I'm ready."

"The leader at Food Watchers says that if I incorporated exercise, I could have a snack or two during the day, and I'm starving for more than a carrot stick." She pulled the bag out of her pocket and dangled them in front of my face. "Yuck." She put them back in her pocket.

Normally, I would smile, agree with her and crack a joke, but this wasn't a joking situation.

She reached out and rubbed my arm, trying to comfort me. "Plus, I want the low-down on if you heard anything about Doug since last night." Bernadine did a couple of warm up moves, reaching her hands up to the sky and then down to touch her toes.

"Come on, Willow." I grabbed her hot pink leash off the kitchen chair and clipped it on her collar. "If you are going to keep up with me, you are going to have to lose some weight too."

Groink, groink.

"I feel your pain," I whispered to her. From her snorts and grunts, I could tell she wanted to walk as much as I did.

We made it around the lake a couple of times. Bernadine yammered on about her divorce and how lucky I would be if it really was Sean that killed Doug, because then he'd be out of my life forever.

I couldn't help but look over my shoulder a time or two. I guess that was a natural reaction when you think someone was setting you up for murder.

"What?" I strained to hear what she was saying. I had to walk twice as fast as Bernadine to keep up. "What did you say?"

"I said that even though I think. . ." She stopped dead in her tracks. She put one hand out to stop me, and the other she put up to her lips. "Shh. Did you hear that?"

Week, week, week, Willow scrambled toward the lake, trying to get away from the sound of breaking twigs in the woods nearby.

"Hold on, girl." I grounded my feet and held on as her leash snapped tight. There wasn't any more slack, and in similar situations I've found myself being dragged behind her while Bernadine flailed her arms.

"Run!" Bernadine screamed, high tailing it out of there without looking back. "Don't kill us!"

Week, week, week. Willow looked back at me as if I couldn't hear the rustling leaves.

I picked up the pace, and practically dragged sweet Willow. *He-hon, he-hon, he-hon,* I pulled so hard that Willow was sliding along the lakebed with her hooves sprawled out on each side.

"Oh, my!" I ran back, picked her up, and took off as fast as one could, holding a seventy-five pound pig in their arms. "I'm so sorry."

We wiggled and jiggled all the way back to the cottage, not looking back. Someone was in the woods, and I wasn't going to find out who it was.

"What took you so long?" Bernadine panted. She was rattling the doorknob trying to get the door open. "Hurry! We have to call Noah!"

"Where's your cell?" On first jab, the key went right in the hole. Kicking the bottom corner of the door, it flung open.

"I left it at home." She ran inside, pushing Willow and me out of her way. "I didn't figure someone was *really* out to kill you."

Willow ran back to the bedroom. Bernadine ran straight to the kitchen where the phone hung on the wall and looked out the window over the sink.

"I bet we can see them." She stretched the phone cord across the counter and strained her neck to see if she could see into the woods.

Honk, honk, honk.

I rolled up on my tiptoes and peered out over her shoulder.

"Park City police. What is your emergency?" The person on the dispatch asked Bernadine.

"I, um. . ." Bernadine muttered.

The gaggle of geese waddled out of the woods from the exact spot where we heard those noises, and straight out to the lake.

"Is there any way we can get some animal control out here by the lake? These geese are taking over." Bernadine stated, pretending to ignore my giggles.

Damn geese.

"I guess I better go, and let you get ready for your day." Bernadine's mood seemed suddenly buoyant.

"I'm afraid my day isn't going to be like I thought it was going to be…say…a week ago." What I wouldn't give for it to be a week ago when I planned on holding bead classes and the Divorced Diva meeting. I wouldn't even mind doing inventory at this point.

"Hey, I've got an idea. Why don't you come to my Food Watchers meeting with me today?"

I'd never even thought about going to a Food Watcher meeting, but the walk did feel good, minus the tiny heart attack the geese gave us.

Maybe I would give it a try to lose a little weight, but I didn't want to commit to anything. My life was already complicated enough without having to try to keep track of what I was eating. These days, I wasn't eating a whole lot.

On second hand, maybe I needed to continue to store up my fat. From what I heard, the food in jail was pretty bland.

"I'll think about it." There was absolutely zero commitment coming from me. "Do they have meetings in the Swanee jail?" I laughed, half kidding, half not.

"You aren't going to jail, Holly. We won't let that happen." She scowled. "I will let you know when the next meeting is and you can go with me." She stretched her arms above her head. "I'll see you tonight at the official Diva meeting."

I made sure that everyone from last night's emergency meeting kept our rescheduled Diva meeting. After all, I didn't want anyone outside our circle thinking we were up to something---like the little sleuthing we were doing.

"Bye, Willow," Bernadine called down the hall, and then opened the door.

The wind whipped around the lake, creating an eerie sound from the trees and echoing down the valley. A flash of panic shot through my heart. When Bernadine left, I'd be alone.

"Let's walk tomorrow too," I said and nonchalantly took a quick look around to see if anyone was outside, watching me.

"Okay, sounds great. I'll see you tonight." She waved goodbye before stepping into her rowboat and heading back to her side of the lake. She hollered over her shoulder, "Call me if you need me. From that dinosaur land-line of yours."

I put away all silly notions that someone was watching me and took a quick shower. I couldn't help but sing a couple lines from Rockwell's 1984 hit, *Somebody's Watching Me*.

I peeked around the shower curtain when the door hinges creaked. Willow was licking up the water that had splashed out.

"When I'm in the shower, I'm afraid to wash my hair," I sang, in my best Rockwell impression. I'd just relaxed, soothed by the steady stream of hot water against my shoulders when the ringing phone caused them to tense up again.

Quickly I shut off the water, and grabbed a towel. If any of the Divorced Divas thought they were going to call and cancel, they were wrong. I had never asked for a favor from them…ever. But now I had called it in and I expected them to deliver.

Noah Druck's voice echoed out of the answering machine into the cottage, and down the hall. "Holly, the police will be coming by the shop to do a onceover, making sure they didn't miss anything. You can open the shop after lunch."

There was a pause.

"We found fudge under Doug's nails. Fudge." He sounded intrigued. "Oh, and don't leave town."

His words played over and over in my mind.

Fudge. Agnes Pearl was the only person in town that made fudge on a regular basis and Marlene always brought it into the shop.

Was that a clue? Doug had done work at Agnes' recently, and he could've gotten some from her at the time. Also, Marlene always carried some with her, and she was talking to Doug that night.

To keep my mind off the possibility that someone in Swanee was setting me up, I cleaned the cottage from top to bottom. Of course it didn't work. Every time I heard as much as a bird chirp, I'd run to my window and look out, not to mention Willow ran under the bed while squealing her little head off. So my mind continued to go over facts about the murder that I knew.

One, Doug's dead body was found on my bead shop floor. Two, whoever did it was definitely trying to make it look like I killed him. Three, I'm scared of geese. Four, fudge was found under Doug's nails, which meant that he had to have been with someone who had fudge, and that wasn't me. And five, I needed to find out if Flora got in touch with Bennie's private investigator.

Careful not to make any fast moves, just in case someone was watching, I shuffled down the hall with my back up against the wall, and then scooted into my bedroom. At least the bedroom window faced out to the barn, which gave me a great view if there was anyone out there.

Grabbing the old rotary, I sat on the edge of the bed and put the cradle in my lap. Keeping one eye on the window and the other eye on the phone, I dialed Flora.

Damned answering machine. Normally I'd hang up, but this situation was far from normal. Every minute I wasted not trying to figure out who was framing me, was a minute closer to my wearing an orange jump suit.

"Flora, I wanted to know if you got in touch with that private investigator yesterday. Noah called and said the police are going to do another once over to make sure they didn't miss something. I was sort of hoping Bennie's guy," I felt my eyes roll, and continued, "got over there and looked around."

Then I called the other Diva's to remind them we were business-as-usual, and insisted they had to be there.

Even Marlene had to be there. I needed to pick her brain, in a nonchalant way, of course, because she already accused *me* of accusing *her*. Plus, we needed to plan a visit to Ginger and the Sloan family to offer our condolences.

None of them answered their phones.

"It must be nice gallivanting around to who knows where with not a care in the world!" I yelled into Cheri's answering machine, after realizing the luxury of galavanting had been stripped from me.

Noah did say *not* to leave town, which I never did anyway, but if I wanted to I didn't have the freedom.

This was worse than being married to Dumb Ass!

I was still going to have to rehash the details to Marlene and Agnes tonight. Not that I wanted to, but Agnes was far from being crossed off my list of suspects. But why would she frame me? Or was she framing Marlene?

There were a lot of questions that were going to be asked tonight and I only hoped that Flora, Cheri, and Bernadine played along as if we hadn't already had our little private meeting last night.

Chills crawled up my spine when I glanced out the window before putting the phone back on the cradle. As if a bad movie was playing right in front of me, an image of

Doug's dead body popped into my head giving me the hebbie-jebbies---It was a picture I'll never be able to forget.

"Shake it off. You are going to be fine. Noah is going to solve this," I whispered while grabbing my yoga pants off the chair next to the bed.

Groink, groink. Willow's snort was deep and billowy.

Who was I trying to convince? Willow or me?

I couldn't go to jail. Not only because I didn't commit the murder, but who was going to take care of my ornery pig?

I slipped on my yoga pants and tugged at the waist. There was little space between my skin and the elastic.

"Hmm." I rolled up on my tippy toes and looked into the vanity mirror.

I noticed a little slack in my derriere. I realized I had forgotten to eat yesterday. As a matter of fact, I'd forgotten to eat this morning, too.

I wanted to lose weight, but not by the Dead Guy Diet.

All the Divas were supposed to be at the shop by 7 p.m. for the Divorced Diva meeting. With all the stress I had had, sitting through a night of beading with Agnes Pearl might just put me under.

Her arthritis was so bad, I wasn't sure she'd be able to hold the wire in order to string the small glass beads. I'd even heard that her eyesight was getting worse, which meant she probably wasn't even going to be able to see the small bead holes.

"Come on, girl." I patted my leg for Willow to come.

Sitting in this house was like a duck waiting to be shot. I had plenty of time to go to the local super center so I could get Agnes some of those wooden bead jewelry-making kits for children. The beads were bigger and so were the holes. If I wasn't mistaken, the string in the kit was actually a shoelace. Those would be perfect for Agnes.

Chapter six

"Stop that." I swatted Willow's nose away from sniffing the bag. She'd love to get her wee-piggy teeth into those wooden beads.

Groink, groink, groink, she looked up at me with her beady black eyes begging for another sniff. She nudged the glove box, wanting me to give her one of the treats that I store in there, and I did.

After getting Agnes' special big hole wooden beads from the store, Willow and I pulled up in front of my darkened bead shop and parked in the empty space. The police tape was gone. The awning flapping in the spring breeze over the front stoop read, The Beaded Dragonfly. On a normal day, the dark shop didn't spook me, but today was different.

Life had to go on, even if Swanee was on edge with the murderer still on the loose. That meant The Beaded Dragonfly's beginning beading class must go on too. Today was the first day of the four week class.

There were ten people enrolled, and the only one who had any experience was Flora. She took every beading class

The Beaded Dragonfly offered. She didn't have anything better to do, other than talk on her phone.

I took a little comfort in knowing Willow was with me. Although I didn't know what she could do if someone attacked me. Willow can't bark like a dog, and she was scared of her own shadow.

With a click of the key, and a flip of the switch, The Beaded Dragonfly came to life with all its brilliant colors bouncing off each other. I was glad to see that the police didn't feel the need to throw that fingerprint dust around again today.

Each glass bead added a different spectrum of color, and a special touch to the shop.

Most of the items I needed for the class were still in the storage closest. I locked the shop door behind me since I had some time before Marlene showed up and we officially opened. Today, she was going to work with any customers while I taught the class.

Oink. Willow gave a snort with one ear perked up.

Oh, no. My eyes widened, and I stopped dead in my tracks waiting listening for any noises. This was Willow's something-is-outside look. She was especially good at hearing things before I did. She always knew when someone was driving up at our cottage before they put their car in park.

The jingle of a door handle echoed throughout the shop and reverberated in my stomach. The sign clearly said 'closed', and someone was definitely trying to get in.

Clunk, clunk, clunk.

Willow darted underneath the wire shelving. Looking around for something to protect me, I grabbed a pair of needle-nose-pliers. They are dull, but pointy. And I could probably do a little damage if I needed to jab someone with them.

I wasn't sure if the rattling door was getting louder, or if was the clattering of my teeth. With the pliers held tight to my chest, I took in a deep breath before I plunged into the shop.

"Good morning. Holly?" Marlene flung her purse in the air just as I came lunging at her, with my tool blazing. "What in the hell are you doing?"

"Ouch, ouch, ouch!" I screamed, as her purse hit me square in the hand, sending the pliers flying across the floor. "What in the world do you have in that thing?"

Click, click, click. Willow ran out of the storage as fast as she could. Once she saw Marlene, she darted under the lowest shelf; only the back half of her didn't fit.

"It's okay." I patted her butt with one hand and shook the other hand, trying to get the sting from Marlene's purse out of it. "You scared the living daylights out of me."

She dangled her keys in the air. Her perfectly shaped eyebrows dipped as she chomped, "I have my own keys, remember?" She looked at me like I had two heads.

"Yeah, well someone killed Doug right over there," I pointed and snarled, "remember?"

I bit my lip. What if I had just pissed her off and she was going to string some cat eyes around my neck?

"Umm. . ." I stumbled, "I'm sorry. I'm just on edge. You can go ahead and start counting out the beads I'm going to need for the class."

On my way back to the storage room to retrieve the beading boards, I picked up the pliers that Marlene had wacked out of my hands with that purse, and gripped them. . .just in case.

Briefly, I turned around and eyeballed her hot pink bag that was lying on the countertop. It was begging for me to peek inside. Screaming, in fact.

"I need to get that purse," I said under my breath, making a mental note, just as I grabbed the ten grey bead boards off the shelf, and then returned to the front of the shop.

Bead boards were the first beading tool I would introduce to the group. It might be a self-explanatory tool, but it was useful for so much more than just laying out your design. The markings allow you to create the perfect-sized bracelet that can cater to anyone, regardless of the thickness of their wrists.

I hopped over what I had begun to think of as 'Doug's spot', and was glad to see Marlene was already working on the to-do list I had given her. She had the window cleaner out, spraying and wiping down the windows and the front door.

It amazed me how dirty they got on a daily basis. You wouldn't think anyone would smear their hands along a window, but they do, and Marlene was the lucky one who has to clean them.

"That Agnes," Marlene said. She shook her head, and then went back to spraying and wiping, every once in a while, using her nails to scrape something off. "She's wearing me out. I really do think she is going blind."

This wasn't a shock. Over the past couple of years, I'd noticed how Agnes' appearance wasn't as "put together" as it used to be.

The Sloans were the wealthiest family in Swanee, but Agnes was the wealthiest widow. She always wore strands of necklaces that started around her neck and finished below her boobs. Her long flowing dresses swept the floor, creating a *swooshing* sound every time she glided into a room. And boy, did she glide. Agnes Pearl had more elegance in her pinky finger than the rest of the citizens of Swanee put together.

As the years passed, and she had gotten older, Agnes' hair began to thin. She'd invested in all sorts of jeweled turbans. Her purple one, with a big red feather sticking out from a jewel on the front, was by far her favorite.

I placed a bead board in front of every empty chair at the two beading tables I had reserved for the class.

"Why do you think Agnes is going blind?" I asked, really glad that Marlene didn't want to talk about Doug. I was tired of talking and hearing about it, even though I did want to find out why someone killed him in my shop, and who the killer was. I eyed her suspiciously.

She was awfully calm if she was the killer.

Marlene tapped the counter with her hot pink acrylic nails and chomped her gum as if she was thinking up a good reason for my question.

"Well?" I asked again, wanting to know the answer. Was Marlene trying to put the wealthiest woman in Swanee in a nursing home? Was Agnes her next victim?

My faith in Marlene was waning.

I walked over to the supply wall and picked out ten pair of pliers and ten crimpers from the tool baskets.

These would do. There were so many tools that I could teach the students to use, but today was the easiest day of class. Using the two most basic tools was the obvious choice to start with.

The pliers were good for holding the wire steady when you finished the bracelet, while the crimpers would secure the bracelet closure with a simple silver crimp tube.

Luckily, today's was a basic lesson on stringing beads and crimping on a closure. Easy.

"This morning she was making a peanut butter and jelly sandwich while I was paying her bills online. Pretty simple, right? No, not for Agnes." Marlene leaned across the freshly cleaned counter with her elbows planted on the glass. I could see the small humidity clouds forming around her wrinkled skin. "She asked me if I wanted one. How hard is it to make peanut butter and jelly sandwiches?"

She grabbed her purse and put it under the counter, out of the way.

"Not too hard." I shrugged, and tried not to make it obvious that I was watching her every single move.

I put pliers and crimpers on each of the bead boards. I wanted to have all the supplies out and ready when they got there.

As simple as the basic bracelet was, it would take me the full hour to go around and check everyone, correct everyone, and even just do the task for some of the students. I had to be fully prepared.

"It was hard. The jelly is in the refrigerator next to the hot salsa." Marlene stood back up and wiped the counter again. "She thought the salsa was the jelly. I took a big bite and nearly fell off the computer chair. I gagged all the way to the bathroom."

I couldn't help but laugh. It certainly wasn't funny that Agnes' health was declining, but I'd have given anything to see Marlene take a chomp of a peanut butter and salsa sandwich. Secretly, I wondered if Agnes hadn't done it on purpose. That was something Agnes would do.

"Agnes didn't even notice the smell when she opened the jar?" She put her purse back on the counter and unzipped it. "No. As a matter of fact, she ate her entire sandwich and mine!" Marlene's eyes were as big as saucers and batting her fake lashes made them look even bigger. "I told her that we needed to call the doctor about getting her eyes examined."

She pulled out a bag of fudge, and held it toward me.

"No thanks." I gulped.

She popped a piece in her mouth, along with her gum, and then put the cleaner in the cabinet behind the counter. She crossed it off her to-do list. She doesn't work every day, but on bead class days it was nice to have someone to help out so I could give my undivided attention to the beaders.

Most of the time, Marlene was would work on her wrapping technique, so she could wrap her fancy yellow diamond Spinel into a piece she could wear on a chain. Or, at least that's what she told me. It was something she didn't tell any of the other Divas, including Agnes.

"At least she has you." I was skeptical of Marlene at first, but not as much as Ginger. Ginger didn't hide the fact that she didn't trust Marlene. Now I'm not so sure Ginger wasn't right.

"I'm happy to help her." Marlene opened one of the new inventory boxes I left out for her to stock. She sat the xacto-knife on the table, next to the box.

If I had to, I could probably grab it before she could get to it.

Stop it, I said over and over in my head. Surely, if Marlene had killed Doug, she'd been long gone by now. There really was nothing keeping her here in Swanee, but that didn't mean I was marking her off my list.

Putting the idea of Marlene as the killer aside, I helped her unpack a little bit of the boxes. There was nothing more exciting than opening up a new box of inventory. All the new designs always got my blood pumping. Opening my own lapidary fed my addiction.

I put handfuls of mismatched beads on each bead board. The students could pick out what they liked from the pile. The bracelets they made today would be nothing like the big project they would have completed by the time the four-week course was over.

"Oh, that's neat," Marlene gasped, holding up a small plastic bag of tied-dyed-looking glass beads.

"Those are Chevron Beads." I took one of the packages out of the box and opened it.

These beads always made me smile. The swirling colors blended so nicely, creating a tie-dyed look. These were especially popular with teenagers. The kids loved to string these, making necklaces, or even putting 8mm sterling silver beads between them. These beads can be worn with anything to complete an outfit.

I put them back and went to get a spool of Accu-Flex wiring for each of the students. There were so many wires used for beading, but I had found that this particular brand of wire held its shape and didn't wear out. If you use cheap wire, the bracelet will break after only a couple days of wearing it. That was not the quality of work or image I wanted The Beaded Dragonfly to be known for.

"These are cool too." Marlene emptied out another bag of beads into the palm of her hand.

"Those are glass components." I picked up a heart-shaped one and held it up to the light. They really do add a touch of class to any bracelet with their sparkle and shine.

I usually suggest using only one component per bracelet, because they're a little pricey.

A knock at the door caused us both to look up. There were a couple of women waiting outside. The older of the two was tapping her watch. It was past ten a.m. and time to open.

I was happy to see that the customers hadn't been scared off because of dead Doug.

"Let's get to work," I hollered over my shoulder before I opened the door, and turned the sign around from closed to open.

"Yeah, yeah." Marlene chomped, but she didn't take her eyes or hands out of the box.

Chapter Seven

"Good afternoon. Welcome to the Beaded Dragonfly." I held the door so the waiting customers could come in. "Can I help you find something?"

"No, thank you." The young girl smiled and pointed over to the counter. The older woman, who I presumed was the mother, didn't look as anxious. If I wasn't mistaken or paranoid, I'd think she was giving me the onceover.

"If you need anything, please let me know." Was I being paranoid? Did everyone in Swanee really suspect that I was the killer?

I eyed the woman back by giving her a friendly smile that wasn't returned on her end. She didn't look like a jewelry beader, but the young one might be, but they went to the counter, which gave a good inclination that they were here to buy.

I was always curious to see who was a beader and who was buyer. They were two completely different kinds of clients. I loved showing people how to bead, but loved the buyer even more. The most lucrative part of owning my own bead shop was designing jewelry for people.

When I first opened the shop, I had a grand vision that women would flock to me to design their next cocktail party necklace, or bead themselves a really cool watch. It had turned out that people wanted to learn how to make their own.

"Oh, look at these!" Marlene continued to inspect every new bead in the box, interrupting me.

The younger customer hurried over to Marlene to see what all the fuss was about, her high, brown ponytail whipped around in circles as she trotted over to eye the beads.

"Oh, Momma!" the girl gasped, her big brown doe-eyes growing wide. "These are perfect."

"Of course they are, dear." The momma leaned my way and her voice dripped with a sarcastic tone. "Everything is perfect in her mind."

The young woman had good taste. The foil-lined glass beads were very popular with brides-to-be, and judging by that chunk of diamond on her ring finger, she was definitely about to walk down the aisle.

I walked over to get Marlene's hands out of the box, so she could finish her to-do list.

"Let me help you with that." I took the new inventory box and sat it behind the counter. "Are you looking for something special?"

Marlene grabbed the box back. She knew she needed to check off the inventory before it could be put out to stock. Most mornings we had time to do that, but not today.

Marlene tiptoed over Doug's spot. She did a little shimmy, almost tipping the beads out of the box.

"Just creeps me out." She held the box with one hand, and circled her free hand over Doug's spot.

I could just see those amazing new beads spilling out and finding a home in *The Under*. That was something I couldn't afford today. I gave her *the look* to shut her up. I might have found a bride client, and I couldn't afford to lose her. In the back of my mind, I had to wonder if Marlene was trying to sabotage my appointment.

"I'm sorry." I turned my attention back to my bride, er, customer.

"I am looking for something really special." She beamed, and wiggled spirit fingers in front of my face. "I need at least sixteen matching bridesmaid necklaces, earrings, and bracelets."

"I think we should not be hasty, Margaret." The mom patted her daughter's hand.

"Oh! You're Margaret McGee." I had heard her name from Ginger quite a few times since Margaret's father, Bear McGee, was the Sloan's lawyer. I had voted for him as the city attorney. I didn't know them personally. Come to think of it, I bet Ginger threw the business my way.

I laid the photo album with pictures of my designs in front of them. I had taken pictures of other items I had designed and made for myself over the years and put them in an album for customers just like Margaret to look at.

A couple more customers came in. I left Margaret and her mom to check it out while I walked over to the others.

"Welcome. Are you here for the beginning beading class?" I asked.

I noticed that they were hanging around the beading tables that I had set up for the class.

I pulled out a couple of the chairs so they could sit down. "Go ahead and get comfortable. We're waiting on a few others."

I walked back over to Margaret and her mom. "Take your time. I'm going to get some refreshments out of the

back for my beading class, so yell if you have any
questions."

"Beading class?" Margaret clapped her hands together;
her high-ponytail flopped to the side. "Momma!"

Momma had better watch her alignment, I thought as
Margaret grabbed her momma's hand and dragged her over
to the beading tables.

"Remember why we are here." Momma stopped dead
in her tracks, reeling in Margaret. "Ms. Harper, we aren't
sure if working with you is a good idea, and I told Margaret
that we needed to come in here and see what type of
establishment The Beaded Dragonfly is."

"I'm sorry. I'm a bit confused." I tilted my head,
squinting my eyes, and trying to figure out what she meant
by "type of establishment."

"You know the murder and all." She covered her
mouth with the back of her hand so no one would hear.

But the whole town already knew about it.

"Momma!" Margaret gasped. "Where are your
manners?"

"Margaret, you know we can't be associated with any
type of criminal activity. Daddy wouldn't approve."
Momma looked me up and down. "I guess it seems like

you're on the up and up. Plus, you don't really look like you could murder someone."

I really wanted to whack her, but I needed this job. I needed the income from sixteen sets of bridesmaids' accessories, so I just bit my lip.

"I can assure you I am on the up and up. I will design and make the most beautiful accessories you've ever seen for a bridal party." I hated to beg, but I would have gotten on my knees if I'd needed too.

"Fine. We will give you a shot." Momma sat down next to Margaret.

"I'm so embarrassed." Margaret flipped her ponytail.

I smiled. It looked like Margaret and her momma were attending the class.

I grabbed a couple more bead boards, and Marlene put the cookies and fruit punch out on the counter. Within ten minutes, all the beaders were there, including Margaret and her momma.

After some small talk and a few refreshments, it was time to start class. The first beading class was always a lot of repetition.

"Hi, thank you all for signing up." I greeted them with a smile and made eye contact with each of them. I didn't want them to think I was hiding anything about the murder. "Not to make light of the situation, but I was afraid that no one was going to show up because of what happened here."

I didn't want to ignore what had happened. No matter how you looked at it, finding a dead guy in your shop couldn't be good for business.

"Over the next four weeks of classes, we will be making a simple beaded bracelet, earrings, and a necklace." All of these were quite simple and added a little difficulty as they progressed to each new accessory. "Today, we are going to learn the basic tools, and how to make a basic bracelet."

I brought out a single-strand glass bead bracelet I had made as an example to pass around to my beginner classes. Seeing examples always helped me when I started beading my own jewelry.

We went through each tool and its purpose. I asked them to use their piles of beads to lay out a design. Each one of them took the time to consider carefully where to place each bead.

Some of them wanted to use fancier beads, but I always saved those for the more advanced classes.

I repeated the process several times, teaching them the proper technique for measuring their wrists. It was hard for them to understand that they had to add an inch to the length, because they had to leave enough space for the crimp and toggle closure. Plus, a little extra wiggle room never hurt anyone.

After they were finished designing their bracelets, I introduced the Accu-Flex wire they would be using to string the beads. Accu-Flex is a great wire that is flexible and sturdy enough that the bracelet can be worn every day. I showed them the bead hole size, and how it compared to the 8 gauge wire I was using.

"I had no idea you had to keep wire size in mind." Zelma, Margaret's momma, fingered the spool of wire, taking a closer look.

For a split second, I wondered why the murderer hadn't used wire to strangle Doug. He or she had actually used the cat eyes that were threaded on wool yarn. That meant that the murderer had to be really strong.

Learning how to crimp one side of the closure proved to be a little difficult for most of the class. It was hard to hold the wire, put the crimp bead on, add the toggle closure, and double the wire over into the crimp bead before you used the crimp tool to finish it off.

"I don't understand why we can't just string them and then put the closure on." Flora had her phone pinned between her ear and shoulder while trying to hold up the wire and string the beads.

"It's much easier for you to string the beads with one end finished." I showed them what I meant by using a bracelet I was working on as an example. "The beads won't fall off, and it's easier to complete."

Each student was at a different skill level. Flora wasn't making any progress, but she did make progress in her phone conversation as she cackled to the person on the other end. I had to hush her a few times.

Margaret was the student who surprised me the most. She was a perfect crimper. It had taken me several tries to get that good of a double fold when I was starting out. Zelma wasn't doing as well.

Every time Zelma pushed her reading glasses up on her nose, she would let go of the open end of her bracelet. She lost several beads to *The Under*. I was glad I had given them the handful of mismatched beads instead of the more expensive ones.

I glanced over at Marlene, who was working the counter as other customers came in. She had Tigertail beading wire wrapped around her pointer finger. She had been working hard on the wrapping technique so she could wrap her yellow Spinel. I had suggested she continue to practice on her finger or other glass beads the size of the Spinel. If she perfected the technique, it would lessen her chances of scratching the precious gem when it was time to wrap it.

She wrapped, unwrapped, and then wrapped again. It was a nice tight fit. Images of the cat eye strand around Doug's neck popped into my head. I shook it off and went back to the group of students.

Everyone put the finishing touches on their bracelets.

"If you wouldn't mind cleaning up your clippings and putting them in the trash, that would be great." I pointed to the trashcans. "And if you don't mind putting your tools away, hang onto your bead boards along with your beads and wire. I have a spot in the storage room for you all to store your projects."

One by one, each student came to me with their bead boards, and I walked them back to the storage room, getting chills every time I walked over Doug's dead spot.

"Feel free to come in between classes and work on your projects or practice." I wanted to encourage them to stop in any time and be able to get their money's worth.

But most importantly, I wanted them to come back more often, which would increase the possibility that they would purchase something.

"Are you okay?" Marlene asked when all the students had left. "You look a little tense."

She was right. I could feel my shoulders creeping up to my ears. I loved teaching class and beading, but I was having a hard time getting the image of Doug's body out of my head, and the wrapping technique she had used around her finger was, well . . .perfect.

"I'm just a little tired." I laughed it off. I didn't want to give Marlene any inclination that she was on my short, very short, list of murderers. "Teaching really takes it out of me."

"Why don't you go home for a little rest before the Divorced Diva's meeting?" Marlene said as she flipped through one of the beading catalogues. "I can hold down the fort for a little bit."

There probably wasn't much Marlene couldn't hold down.

"Thanks. I think I'll take you up on that offer." I went back to the office to retrieve Willow and we headed for home.

Chapter Eight

I could see that the building where the Food Watchers group meets was all lit up as I was on my way home.

With Marlene finishing up at the shop, I'd thought taking a walk with Willow would be just the thing I needed to relieve my stress and help me get ready for tonight's Diva meeting. But then, I thought that Bernadine might be right. Food Watchers was at least worth a shot.

I whipped my little VW into the parking lot. It wasn't going to hurt to check it out. I pulled out Willow's travel water bowl and put it on the floorboard. After cracking the window so she'd get some air, I headed in to face the scale.

The meeting was located in one big room with ten rows of yellow chairs. There were three workstations with computers and floor scales along with a Food Watcher Specialist in matching yellow shirts and khaki pants.

"Hi, there." Enthusiasm oozed from the size zero Food Watcher Specialist. "Are you new?" She chirped this in a voice that indicated she might bring out the 'spirit hands' at any moment.

At that moment, everyone sitting in the yellow chairs rotated and looked at me as if I was on display. I bet they could smell a new member a mile away.

Charlie was the name printed on the tag pinned to the specialist's shirt.

"Hi, Charlie." I smiled and nodded.

"Holly!" Bernadine jumped up from the front row and waved her arms while walking over. "I'm so glad Marlene caught you."

"Caught me?" I drew back, trying to figure out what she was talking about.

"Excuse me, she's with you?" Charlie clasped her hands in delight. It was a little too much delight, if you asked me.

"She is," Bernadine broke out in a singsongy voice. "Yes, she is."

Charlie took a small steel hammer and hit a bell attached to the edge of her desk. *Ding! Ding! Ding!* Everyone cheered. I just wanted to hide.

Bernadine gave Charlie a high-five and then hugged me. "I've been waiting to get my bell."

Charlie took out a bell-shaped lapel pin and fastened it to Bernadine's cardigan. Bernadine touched it with obvious pride.

"If you bring in a new customer, they give you a bell." Bernadine caressed her pin. "Sort of like the saying about an angel getting its wings. When we bring someone new in, we are like angels of weight loss."

Please. I rolled my eyes.

"Whatever." I sighed. "Charlie, I'm really just here to check out the place and see if it's for me." I turned to Bernadine and whispered under my voice, "What was that about Marlene catching me?"

Charlie walked around the counter, never once taking her eyes off me.

"Um. . .what are you doing?" A little anxiety knotted in my gut.

Without a word, Charlie slapped a big 'My Name Is' sticker right across my chest.

"Everyone wears a name tag." Sarcasm dripped from her perfect lips.

To keep the peace, I bit my lip and followed Bernadine to the front of the room, but not without many congratulations for the bell ringing ceremony. Marlene beamed with pride, while I beamed with a red, embarrassed face.

"I called the shop to let you know there was a Food Watchers meeting tonight. She said that you'd just left and she'd try to catch you before you pulled out."

I wasn't going to explain that Marlene hadn't caught me.

"If you had a cell, I could've just called you instead of having to tracking you down." She patted the chair next to her so I would sit down.

I started to ask, "Do we have to sit so close?" but I was interrupted.

"Is everybody ready?" A loud voice boomed over the intercom.

Bernadine and all the other Food Watchers stood up and clapped. A few even let fly with some loud hoots.

Every single person had a beatific smile on their face, as if some Hollywood megastar had just walked into the room.

I craned my neck to see what everyone was so excited about. The clapping and swaying was infectious. Raucous music was blaring and the strobe light in the center of the room rotated, making it hard to focus on anyone.

My toes began to tap like they had a mind of their own. *Well, a little sway too and fro isn't going to hurt anyone* I thought *When in Rome.*

The Food Watchers in the center aisle parted as a tall, blonde, gazelle-like woman made her way through the crowd. She held a microphone in one hand and greeted her eager, food-deprived acolytes with the other.

She had to be the famous "Ms. Food Watchers."

"Hello!" She smiled when she got to the front of the room and hopped up on the small stage right in front of Bernadine and me.

I had to shield my eyes from the glare of her pro-white dentals.

"Is everybody ready to lose some weight?" Ms. Food Watchers pumped her fists in the air and the crowd erupted in even louder cheers.

Just then, something occurred to me. I leaned over and whispered in Bernadine's ear, "This is a cult."

"Shut up, Holly." Bernadine touched her bell pin and continued to clap along with everyone else.

The meeting itself really wasn't so bad, but the enthusiasm of the leaders and members was almost unbearable. No one had said a negative word about food until Ms. Food Watcher mentioned fudge.

A collective gasp filled the room.

"Fudge is not your friend," Ms. Food Watcher whispered as if it was going to help soften the blow for all the fudge lovers in the audience. Then she patted her thighs.

"She better not tell Agnes Pearl." Bernadine cackled.

Agnes Pearl. Fudge. Doug Sloan.

"I'll see you at the Divas meeting," I said to her and jumped to my feet.

"Yes!" Ms. Food Watcher pointed to me. I froze like a deer in headlights when she waved for me to join her on the stage. "You have let the words move you! Everyone on your feet!"

Me? I pointed to myself.

"Yes, you, Holly!" Ms. Food Watcher yelled into the microphone after straining to read the name tag plastered across my chest. "Tell us what moved you."

I glared at Bernadine, who was smiling from ear to ear. She was going to get an earful about this later.

The room went silent. Everyone was waiting to hear what I was going to say.

"I, um. . .realized that fudge is bad." I stood still, but not for long.

Everyone cheered and clapped just like Oprah's audience on her "Favorite Things" show.

"Thank you. Thank you." I held my hands in the air as I casually made my way down the center aisle and straight out the door.

What was that? I couldn't wait until I saw Bernadine at the Divas meeting. I was going to kill her.

Maybe Marlene wasn't the killer. What if it was Agnes? After all, she did threaten to kill Doug, and she could be framing Marlene for it.

Chapter Nine

Willow and I didn't have enough time to make it home and get to the meeting on time, so we went back to the shop. I knew Marlene had probably already closed up and gone to pick up Agnes.

The apartment above the shop was dark. If the light had been on in Cheri's apartment, I would've gone up there and waited, but it wasn't. She must have been at school. Or, better yet, maybe she was at the Livin' End trying to get some scoop on the whole Doug situation.

With Willow on my heels, I crept up the steps. Hesitating for a moment before I pushed the key into the lock, I looked up and down Main Street to see if anyone was around.

My mind was creating havoc.

After barely opening the door, I stuck my hand in and patted up the wall until I found the light switch.

I didn't have enough time to take Willow off her leash before Flora was there, standing outside, talking on her phone—as usual. Her wavy hair was pulled back in a loose ponytail at the nap of her neck.

She waved, and I waved back. Knowing she was there made me feel a little more at ease, and I was able to go in the storage room and retrieve the Divas' bead boards.

I jumped over the spot where I'd found Doug and opened the door. On the far wall, was shelving where Cheri had stored all their projects.

Carefully, one by one, I took each project down, making sure the beads didn't roll off and into an *Under*.

I smiled at Flora's bohemian chandelier earrings. They reminded me of the one thing I'd wanted in my divorce from Sean. His grandmother had given him the most beautiful chandelier. A real chandelier; not just any old light. It was adorned with the most beautiful crystal beads in all shades of pink and red. I had no clue about its monetary value. I just knew that I loved it because of its beading elements.

I lowered my standards and begged him to let me have it for the shop. I even went as far as offering to let him off the hook for alimony for six months, but he refused. He said I could have it when I pried it out of his cold, dead fingers. The beautiful heirloom was sitting in a box in his family room. It would've looked perfect hanging in the middle of my shop.

Anyway, I tried to talk Flora out of making those chandelier earrings since they would be pressed up against that damn phone of hers all the time. I even suggested she get rid of the dang phone, but she gave a resounding, "Hell no!"

Flora was already sitting at the table, chatting it up with Cheri and Bernadine, when I walked back into the shop.

I stopped and looked. For a moment, everything seemed normal, but it wasn't.

"Do you need some help or a hug?" Cheri's beret was sitting sideways on her head. I tried to straighten the crooked hat. She pulled away. "Stop. It's supposed to be that way."

"I'll take the hug." I wrapped my arms around my upstairs tenant.

I was grateful that Cheri hadn't been home when the murder occurred. She'd been spending long hours at the library preparing for her upcoming exams.

Cheri bent down and scratched behind Willow's ears. Willow's tail whirled around in excitement. She loved Cheri, because Cheri was always taking her on quick walks when I was working long hours in the shop. It was a good excuse for Cheri to take a break from studying.

"You're looking fit." Flora commented on Cheri's toned arms.

Cheri flexed. We laughed.

"I've been going to a self-defense class, and it's getting me into shape." She flexed her muscles. "You gals should think about it. Especially now, with a murderer on the loose."

She did have a point. It was something I was going to have to seriously think about. Not only for self-defense, but the toned arms was something I'd always dreamed of having.

I did my little hop over Doug's dead spot and went back to get Cheri's project. It was a stretchy bracelet made from all sorts of different colored glass beads. Nothing too fancy, but she didn't have time to get too involved because of her commitment to school.

When I came back in, I sat her board down and I noticed Marlene helping Agnes up the shop's two front steps. Agnes was smacking Marlene's hands away like she didn't need Marlene's help, when she clearly did.

"Hi, Agnes. You look great." I tried not to focus on her blue hair.

I quickly went back and got another bead board while they got settled in and put Agnes' children's beads on it. It would be a simple single strand of all wooden beads. The package contained beads of various colors, as well as plain, unpainted wood. I'd let her choose which ones to use.

Agnes Pearl was rarely seen without her purple turban, but today she was just sporting her cotton candy blue hair. In fact, I was pretty sure if a child came into the shop, she might try to eat Agnes' hair.

"Thank you, Holly." She pushed her glasses up on her nose. "I thought you looked like you'd lost weight, but it was just the way my glasses were sitting."

"Nice to see you." I smiled politely, setting the board down in front of her.

Without anyone noticing, I slipped my finger back to my elastic waistband to make sure I wasn't delusional from the lack of sleep this morning when I noticed slack in my yoga pants.

Sigh. There was still a little extra space. Although it was small, it was still there.

There were a lot of unflattering things I could have
said in reply to Agnes, but I kept my mouth shut. You
never know what could happen if she turned up dead. Then
I'd be a suspect in two murders. Or better yet, she'd murder
me.

I jumped over Doug's dead spot again to grab Marlene
and Bernadine's projects. There wasn't any sense in
bringing out Ginger's. There's no way she'd come to the
Divas impromptu meeting. I'd left her a message when she
hadn't answered her phone.

I just hoped she didn't think I killed her brother.

"I think it's so good how you gals got this group
together. Those men can be jerks." Agnes sure wasn't
wasting time starting the bashing session. It probably
would've been a good one, but with dead Doug weighing
on everyone's mind, nobody even answered Agnes.

Bernadine carefully laid out her Swarovski crystals in
a pattern. She'd been working in this for the last three
weeks, since we started this new project. Our projects
usually take about a month to complete, and then we move
on. Each Diva had picked out a new technique for the
current project, which meant it was going to take us longer
than normal to complete.

"What do you think?" Bernadine asked, referring to her project.

This was the third pattern she'd laid out. Some with ornamental Bali beads and some she'd replaced with sterling silver.

"I think you set me up!" I said as I glared at Bernadine.

She was crazy if she thought I was going to let her off the hook after the stunt she pulled only an hour before at Food Watchers.

"Me?" Her wide-eyed innocence was merely a smoke screen. "You're the one who jumped up and got the attention of. . ."

I interrupted her, "Ms. Food Watcher!"

All the other Divas looked at us.

Cheri was the only one brave enough to ask, "What happened?"

After I told them the quick story about the nutty scene that had taken place at Food Watchers, a wave of laughter rippled through the group. When the laughter quieted down for a second, Flora couldn't resist.

She stood up and walked over to Bernadine. She bent down and to examined Bernadine's cardigan. "Well, where's that new bell pin, Angel?"

Flora threw her head back and cackled. It was contagious and everyone started laughing all over again.

"Okay." I had to get the Divas back in line. I looked over Bernadine's shoulder at her bracelet. "I like it."

Of course I liked it. I liked anything beaded. My opinion really didn't matter anyway. She was going to take it apart a million more times before she put the final crimp on it. Most of Bernadine's time was taken up by organizing and reorganizing. That was her specialty.

"Have you talked to Ginger?" Marlene asked as she handed me her project.

She had the gauge wire wrapped around her finger instead of the fake gem I'd given her to use. Gently, I reached over to help pull it off and show her how to wrap from the beginning…again.

I wish she'd tell the other Divas about the rare yellow Spinel diamond she wanted to wrap into a new creation so she could wear it. She said it wasn't anyone's business but her own, and it wasn't my story to tell, even though it would've been a wonderfully juicy gossip topic for the Divas to discuss.

"No." I watched over Marlene's shoulder to make sure she was rewrapping the fake gem correctly this time. "I left her a message, but she hasn't called back."

"How do you know she hasn't called? You don't have a cell phone and you're not home to see if she's called," Flora chirped from the other side of the table.

"No thank you. I don't need a cell phone." I reached over Marlene's shoulder to help her with the wire twist. "Besides, I have the shop phone."

Ginger had never hesitated to call the shop before.

"Do they know who killed him yet?" Marlene asked.

"No, but I think Noah suspects me," I said, thinking this was a great time to begin my nonchalant line of questioning about Marlene and her night at The Livin' End.

After all, she was the last one seen talking to him that night.

Marlene dropped the wire and the fake gem on the bead board. Several 6mm sterling silver beads flew up in the air.

I watched the beads fall to the ground as if in slow motion.

"No!" I fell to my knees and reached out on the floor to stop them. "Damn that Spinel!"

It was too late. The beads had bounced right into *The Under*.

"Spin what?" Agnes asked as she tucked her hair behind her ear, exposing her lime green hearing aids. She nudged Marlene. "Can you turn this dang thing up? I can hardly hear the gossip."

Marlene glared down at me. I'd completely let it slip, and leave it to Agnes Pearl to actually hear it.

Marlene hadn't told the other Divas about her rare yellow Spinel diamond yet. She was determined to cover the gem with a wrap. There was no way I was going to risk her scratching it, so that's why I had her working with the fake one.

"Sorry, Holly." Marlene bent down and looked into *The Under*. "I'm sure you can get them later."

She leaned in close to my ear. Her leopard print pencil skirt seams were taut and looked like they were about to rip.

"Keep your mouth shut," she whispered through her gritted teeth.

Marlene got up and straightened her skirt before she eased back into her chair.

"What did she say about a sep something?" Agnes asked again.

Damn, she wasn't going to let it go.

"What?" I played dumb. "Oh, let me fix that."

I took her shoestring and knotted the end around one large bead so the rest wouldn't fall off as she added more beads. Agnes' hands shook as she tried to steady a green wooden bead.

"Why do they make these darn things so small?" She held it right up to her glasses.

I hadn't realized how bad Agnes' eyesight had become. She was always so fun to be around. She still looked exactly the same as she had twenty years ago, except for the blue hair.

"Where did you get your hair done?" I held one of the big beads up for her to put the shoestring through the hole. "It looks nice."

"Marlene, dear." Agnes smiled as the bead glided down the string.

"What did you do?" I mouthed Marlene's way.

"She made me buy that hair color at the drug store." Marlene shook her head. "I tried to tell her, but she wouldn't listen."

"I pay you to take care of me. That means my hair and what I want." Agnes attempted another bead, this time on her own.

I moseyed over to check on the chandelier earring project, but Flora had been too busy catching up on the latest gossip from her sister.

Everyone was working away and silent. Doug was weighing heavily on all our minds.

"Do you think we should take some food over to Ginger's?" I asked, breaking the silence.

It wasn't unusual in Swanee for friends and neighbors to help out by providing food for the family when there is a death. Everyone made sure the family was fully stocked up on food. It was one less thing the family would have to worry about.

"I thought we could all meet up and pay our respects." I touched the beautiful crystal selection on Bernadine's bead board.

I had to see Ginger, and the Divas might be a good excuse for me not to go alone.

"You want to go?" Cheri cocked her head to the side and looked at me like I had two heads. "I mean, he was found dead here in your shop."

"I didn't kill him. And yes, I want to go see my best friend," I confirmed.

Was it that unreasonable to want to go? Did Ginger really think I could've killed Doug?

"All Cheri is saying, is that it might not be the right time to show up if you haven't talked to her yet." Bernadine rearranged the silver and Bali beads on her board for the umpteenth time.

"You don't think I killed Doug?" I placed my hand on my chest.

It's a question I didn't think I had to ask my friends, but evidently, I couldn't be sure. Why would they even be here if they thought I was the killer?

"Why would I kill him?" I begged for an explanation. "And if I did, why would I leave him here? Give me a little more credit, would you"

I had to admit that I'd killed Sean in my mind quite a few times, but I've never left him anywhere that would make me the suspect.

Agnes sat straight up and chimed in. "Well, if Doug was dead, Sean would get more work and your alimony would be paid up and on time."

I was floored. My mouth automatically shot open and then closed. I had called the impromptu meeting to pick Marlene's brain, not for my friends to accuse me of murder.

Chapter Ten

"Don't move," Cheri said suddenly. "I swear I just saw someone looking in the window." She had turned as white as a sheet and she was visibly trembling.

She was pointing towards the front windows with the hand that was holding her bracelet. Her hand was shaking so much that we could hear the beads clicking together.

Right away, we all turned to look out the windows.

"I said not to look." Cheri picked up her pliers as if she was going to stab someone.

"Are you sure you saw someone?" Agnes squinted as if she could really see out into the dark night.

I had to give her an "A" for effort to fit in.

"Always be aware of your surroundings." Cheri said as she walked cat-like toward the window. "Eek!"

When a shadow popped up and looked in the window, Cheri's pliers went flying through the air and she ran in the opposite direction. No words were spoken as Bernadine, Flora, Marlene, and I frantically raced to the storage room, leaving Agnes behind.

"Get Agnes," I said through gritted teeth to Marlene. "You're supposed to be taking care of her."

"Call the cops!" Flora screamed at the top of her lungs.

We all turned and stared at her in disbelief. The one time we needed her to have her phone, and she didn't have it planted between her ear and shoulder.

"What?" She pulled back from our huddle in confusion.

"Where is your phone?" I asked.

"I left it on the table." Flora pointed, and we all looked into the shop.

Agnes was still trying her hardest to string one of those big wooden beads on a shoestring, oblivious to what was going on.

"I left mine on the table, too," Marlene said, chomping away on her gum.

"Me too." Cheri confirmed.

"Mine is in my purse, hanging on the chair," Bernadine said through chattering teeth.

"Somebody get the door." Agnes yelled over her shoulder. "Where'd you gals go?"

Agnes got up before we could stop her and had the door unlocked and wide open.

"Sorry, we're closed." Agnes came face to face with the peeping tom.

She went to shut the door, but it was pushed back open by the other person. We drew in a breath as we heard footsteps that weren't Agnes'. We held our collective breath in anticipation of what was about to happen.

"I'm looking for the Divorced Divas' group," A woman said as she stepped into the light. "I heard they held their meetings here."

We walked back into the shop when we were convinced the five-foot woman with her brown hair styled in a bob wasn't going to open fire.

"Yes, we do meet here." I walked up behind Agnes.

"Now you all come out." Agnes shook her head and walked away. "Chickens."

"With a murderer on the loose, you can never be too sure." Cheri picked her pliers up and then put them back down on the bead board.

"How can we help you?" I asked looking into her red-rimmed eyes.

"I'm getting a divorce, or I think I am. I'm looking for a support group to help me get through it." She dropped her head and looked at her long thin fingers. She played with her simple wedding band. "I'm Sadie May."

"You've come to the right place, honey." Bernadine wrapped her arms around Sadie.

Flora got Sadie some tissues.

"What did your no-good soon-to-be ex do?" Cheri patted the chair next to her for Sadie to sit down."

Sadie sat and melted down into a full, inconsolable sob.

"Now, now, dear." Agnes Pearl assumed her grandmotherly role. "Men are like commercials. You can't believe a word they say."

Sadie's light blue eyes were watery, but a smile crossed her face. "I knew I could count on you Divas to cheer me up." She dabbed her eyes, and then tucked a strand of her short hair behind her ear.

"Tell us, what did he do?" Flora asked.

She had to get the full scoop. I leaned in, and Bernadine eased her chair a little closer to make sure she was within earshot. This was the stuff we Divas live for. Juicy gossip.

"I think he's cheating on me." There was uneasiness in her voice.

"Think or know?" I asked. "Because you are getting divorced."

"Huh?" Cheri's nose curled up.

"Have you already filed for divorce or you just planning on filing?" I asked again. This all sounded very much like it was in the early stages.

"No." Softly Sadie answered. "He doesn't know that I think he's cheating."

"Hold up!" Agnes Pearl put her hands in the air to stop all the talking. "You mean to tell us that you only suspect him and you want to be a Divorced Diva?"

"Yeah, *Divorced* Diva." Flora made sure Sadie understood that you had to be divorced to join the group.

Unless you were Ginger, of course.

"Sadie, he might not really be cheating." I tried to comfort her. Obviously she needed a friend to talk to. "What do your friends think?"

I don't have any." She frowned. "We just moved here for his job and he's always working."

Sadie used finger quotes on "working."

"Just because he's working a lot doesn't mean he's cheating." I assured her. "I'm no detective, but I have been cheated on, and I can smell a cheater from a mile away. This doesn't sound like a cut-and-dried cheating situation."

"Good. So I can count on you to help me?" Sadie's tears had dried up lickity-split.

"What?" I wasn't volunteering for anything. What little time I did have was going toward exonerating myself, The Beaded Dragonfly, and Sean of murder.

"Since you said you were the expert, you just need to see him, right?" Sadie looked for any hope that I'd say yes.

"Why don't you call us back when you have some real evidence that he's cheating. Then we can go from there." I scribbled the phone number down for The Beaded Dragonfly and sent Sadie on her merry way.

Agnes got up and gathered her belongings.

"I think that girl has done fell off the tater wagon." She motioned for Marlene. "Let's go home. That Salsa With The Stars show is on tonight, and I don't want to miss it."

Marlene rolled her eyes and chomped her gum. "We don't want you to miss anything, Agnes."

That was everyone's cue to get their own stuff and head home. We'd had a long day and night.

"We're meeting at Ginger's tomorrow morning." I confirmed it with everyone. "Marlene, are you set to work?"

Marlene was going to cover for me at the shop while I paid my respects. There was no way Marlene was going to set foot in Ginger's house. Ginger didn't like her, and she may have been dating Doug when he died.

"You can count on me," Marlene said, as she helped Agnes down the stairs. Agnes tried to bat her hands away again and Marlene smacked her hands right back.

I shook my head. This was a crazy bunch of Divas, but they were my kind of kooky.

Chapter Eleven

"I'll help you clean up." Cheri picked up a couple of the bead boards off the table, being careful to stack the Diva's projects on top of each other. Briefly, she paused and stood in front of me. "I think we should go to the Livin' End together. Tonight."

"Tonight?" I looked up at the clock on the wall behind the counter. "It's 10:15pm."

"I bet things are really getting started about right now." Her eyes lifted. "People have already had a little time to get a drink or two in them. And you know that saying about alcohol and talking."

I shook my head. "No, I don't know any sayings," I confirmed.

"You should know it." She bit her lip as though she was searching her brain for something. "I don't know what it is, but my aunt, who is about your age, used to say it." She tapped her chin. "Something about having loose lips."

I rolled my eyes. "I don't know. I thought that you could go and report back to me. Not me go with you."

That was the plan. I wanted her to do her sweet college girl thing and fast-talk to get what we needed to get.

"Come on. It'll be fun." She pleaded, following me back to the storage room.

One-by-one I took the boards from her and stacked them back on the shelf for the next meeting.

"I can't do that. Everyone will know what I'm up to."

"I was thinking that you could dress differently." She cast her eyes up and down my body. "I have some stretch pants and a really cool top you can put on. I also have this great wig that we can disguise you in."

"No." I shook my head continually. "That doesn't sound like a very good plan."

"Are you kidding me?" Her mouth formed an O and she stomped the ground. "That's a great idea. Think about it. We can be sitting there like two college girlfriends and you bring up the subject. Instead of me trying to come up with questions on my own, you can ask the questions that you need the answers to."

She did have a point. Just say that I did go in disguise, I could ask any questions and get the information first hand, not second, which was what would happen if Cheri went on her own.

"Fine," I agreed.

"Come on!" Cheri grabbed my hand and pulled me out of the storage room. "Get Willow and lock up. Meet me upstairs."

"Okay. I'll lock up." I showed her out the door, and then went back to the counter.

Placing my hand on the phone, I knew I needed to make a phone call, but wondered if Noah had put a tap on it. Still, I needed to get a hold of Sean. He hadn't returned any of my calls, which made me believe it was a little suspicious.

Before I really had time to think about what I was doing, we were walking into the Living' End. She was right. The bar was hopping.

Cheri wove in and out of the crowd like a true champion. She scored a couple of bar seats at the far end. By the time I waddled over, she had already ordered our drinks and was talking to the guy next to her.

"Here she is." She put her hands out like she was Vanna White and showing me off. "This is Steve. He's a regular here."

Steve nodded, but didn't take his eyes off of Cheri.

"Nice to meet you." I planted a half grin on my face, afraid to smile too much or all the makeup Cheri had put on me would crack off in chunks.

He still didn't look at me. I wouldn't look at me either. There was nothing worse than feeling like a stuffed sausage link, except for looking like one. My legs definitely looked like one, especially with the size-six ankle boots she made me wear, when I wear a size nine shoe.

Pulling the "cool" shirt, which was a cropped sweater with a long tank underneath, down to cover what little it did, I plopped on the bar stool.

"What can I get you?" The bartender asked. He didn't recognize me. Usually he would ask how Sean was, but he didn't this time.

"I'll have water," I stated confidently in my new accent.

Cheri wagged her finger in front of me. "No she won't. She'll have a bourbon and coke." She shooed the bartender off and turned toward me. "What's wrong with your voice? Be cool. Ask questions. Don't make it complicated."

Eric Clapton's Wonderful Tonight echoed all over the bar, and the smoke hung over the pool tables like an early morning fog. I didn't recognize anyone, which I guess was a good thing.

"You come here much?" The guy next to me asked. His button down was untucked and the two top buttons were undone, not to mention it was a little wrinkled. It looked like he had a small stain on the thigh of his khaki pants. The bar light reflected off his bald head.

"No," I stated.

"What are you drinking?" He leaned closer and titled his glass so the ice would clink against the sides.

Cheri elbowed me, giving me the eye.

"I just ordered a bourbon and coke." It was painful to fake a smile. I wasn't good at flirting. I never had been and never would be. Sean and I had known each other for years, so it was a comfortable relationship where I didn't have to try so hard. Maybe I should've. "Do you come here a lot?"

"Not really, but I do love a cute redhead." He fluttered his eyebrows like Groucho Marks.

"What?" I drew back, thinking this man was crazy.

"Your red hair." He pointed to the wig that I had completely forgotten I was wearing. "I like your hair."

"Oh, it's so loud in here that I can hardly hear you." I brushed the edges of the short fake strands with my fingertips. "Thank you so much." I drew out the 'you' in my best southern accent.

I had always heard that men loved southern women, so why not throw that in.

"Cheers." I held my glass up and let him think that I was all into him. I leaned a little closer, and cozied up to him. If I was going to get some information, I was going to have to do this flirting thing. "Did you hear about that big brawl that took place here the other night where one of the men ended up dying?"

"Darling, I sure did hear about that." His lips parted into the widest grin. "From what I hear, there was a little tension between the two. In fact, I'd bet he was having an affair with that bead store owner."

"No he wasn't!" I jumped up, knocking the stool on the ground. Cheri bounced off her seat, ready to pounce.

"What's wrong?" Cheri came nose-to-nose with the guy. "Did you say something to my friend?"

"Cheri?" Someone called from behind us. "Is that you?"

We both turned around. Bernadine stood with her hands on her hips, red hair flowing over her shoulders, and her mouth gaped open. Amusement flickered in her eyes when she noticed me.

"Holly?" Her eyes darted back and forth between me, Cheri, and the guy. "Ernie?"

"Ernie?" Cheri and I asked in unison.

"Yes." He turned completely around on his stool, bald head shining like the North Star.

"I think I'm going to need a drink for this explanation." She pushed her way between us and planted her tush on my stool. Putting her finger in the air, she ordered, "Whiskey sour, please. And make it a double."

"This is Ernie?" My voice dripped with disgust. "He believes that I'm having an affair with Doug."

I glared at him, not taking my eyes off him for one second.

"Was." Ernie lifted his brows, exposing his beady little eyes. "He's dead. Remember?"

"Oh!" I lunged toward him, Cheri pulled me back and my wig went flying off and smacked him square in the face.

"I knew you weren't a real red head." He threw the wig on the bar floor and turned back around in his seat.

"Aw, shut up." I took another seat at the bar. There were plenty to choose from because my little fiasco had scared everyone off. The bartender shot my glass down the bar with a look of death. "Sorry."

"What is going on here?" Bernadine got off her stool and grabbed the wig. "If I knew you wanted to be a redhead like me, I would've given you the name of my hair dresser." She shook her head, her curls flying back and forth.

"Funny," I murmured. "You know I asked Cheri to come here to find out what happened. She had this *great* idea that I should come here in disguise and hear from the regulars myself."

"Really?" Cheri tipped her face and chuckled. "I didn't realize that you were going to pick a fight...like Sean."

"Okay, let's not get feisty." Bernadine stood up next to us. "It was a good plan, but you talked to the wrong guy. I told you that I would talk to Bennie's PI. I wasn't going to meet him alone, so meeting here was a good place to start."

"Listen, I'm just here to make a buck." He picked up his drink glass and tilted it toward me with his finger pointing at me. "I never intended to meet up with a fake red head."

"Oh shut up." I swung my head around Bernadine to see him. "I don't want you investigating anything."

"Great!" Ernie tossed back his drink and slammed down the glass along with a wad of cash. "I've got real innocent people to help." Knocking back his stool, he walked out.

"Oh, Ernie, don't leave." Bernadine called after him. When he didn't turn around, she did. "Now we don't have a PI, Holly."

"Who cares? He already had me convicted." I hung my head, and laughed out loud when I looked down at the outfit I was wearing. "Look at me! Who am I kidding?"

"What are you talking about?" Cheri shook her head, and spoke in a slightly bitter tone.

"I'm here in your size two clothing, trying to look hip and desperately looking for a killer that is framing me." I shuddered in humiliation, and then broke out in tears. "When in reality, I'm just pathetic. I'm going to jail."

"No!" Cheri and Bernadine surrounded me.

"Don't think like that." Cheri hugged me. "We are going to figure this out."

"That's right." Bernadine nodded. Her determination didn't falter. "We Divas always figure out everything."

Bernadine was right. We did always figure out any sticky situations we ever got in, but never murder.

Chapter Twelve

The next day, before I headed over to the Sloan's with a veggie tray from the grocery store, I decided to give Sean a call.

Surely, he'd heard the news about Doug, and I was a bit surprised he hadn't returned my calls.

We might be divorced, but he was still the nosiest man I'd ever known. He also felt he had a vested interest in The Beaded Dragonfly because he was paying me alimony, which was never on time nor in full.

"Sean, it's Holly." I said to his answering machine. "I need to talk to you. Please call me back. And it's not about the alimony being late."

I had to finish big because it was time to pay up and that's generally the only time I called him.

I wondered where he was working this week. If I knew, I'd drive by after I gave my condolences to Ginger.

There was no parking on Main Street when I drove by the Sloan's old Victorian house. There were people going in and out of the wrought-iron fence gate piled high with tin-foiled goodies. Parking at The Beaded Dragonfly was at a premium and I had Willow with me. I could park, check on the shop and walk back down Main Street to Ginger's place.

The shop was safe and sound and I left Willow on the couch in the office. I checked the time, noting that Marlene would be there at any moment to open for me.

As I stepped over the spot where I found Doug, a chill went up my spine, just to think that a couple days ago, someone stood on this very spot and killed someone with a strand of my beads. Not to mention, they were trying to peg me as the murderer.

A couple of chattering women Walked into the shop and Willow ran toward them.

"I'm sorry." I patted my leg for Willow to stop sniffing them. "We aren't open this morning."

The sign on the door was still flipped to display the closed side.

I wasn't really afraid of offending them. The two plump women had been coming into the shop for about three months, and had never bought a single bead.

Without a word, they left and didn't even look back.

I grabbed an open bag of chocolate chip crumbs and headed out the door.

The old Victorian house had been passed down the Sloan's for generations. Lucky Ginger was now the proud owner, and was living in the creepy old mansion. Thank God, there wasn't a clause in the will that stated the house had to stay the same, because Ginger had every room's wallpaper stripped and painted and had replaced all the old cherry wood crown molding with white.

I peered into the parlor where everyone seemed to be gathering. Ginger spent most of her time there and today was no different. She was perched in the same high-back chair she always sat in. Leave it to Ginger to be all dolled up when she knew company would be coming. She always dressed like the artsy type, lots of layers, scarves, and dangling earrings. Her thick dark hair hung in long graceful curls around her shoulders and her hands lay delicately in her lap holding a few tissues.

I ran my hands through my dull brown bobbed-hair and pushed a stray strand behind my ear. I tugged the hem of my shirt to cover up the frumpy elastic-waist jeans I'd found at the local dollar shop.

When she blotted her eyes, she noticed me standing in the doorway.

She got up to greet me, the scarves delicately floating behind her, and said, "Oh, Holly, can you believe it?" Ginger's eyes grew big.

I let out a small "eek" from the four small indentions she made into the flabby side of my upper arm as her nails dug into my flesh. I gripped the veggie tray tighter so I wouldn't drop it and send veggies flying everywhere, with no Willow there to clean it up.

"Follow me." There was urgency in her voice.

I tried to jerk away from her grip, but she had a vice-like hold and if I jerked too much, my skin would rip off. She nodded to the crowd of people gathered in the hallway while I spat out the tips of her scarves that were finding their way into my mouth. She dragged me into the guest bathroom and locked the door behind us.

The bathroom was bigger than my entire cottage. Ginger flung her back on the shut door and ordered me to sit in the vanity chair.

"Okay, spill the beans." Ginger narrowed her eyes. "Who bought them?"

"Bought what?" She didn't leave me time to tell her how sorry I was to hear about Doug.

I held the veggie tray in front of me. She took it and put it on the vanity.

"The strand of black cat eyes. Who bought them?" Ginger asked.

I nearly jumped out of my elastic waistband pants when someone pounded on the door.

"Ginger, are you in there?" Flora's voice came from the other side of the door.

"Um, hmm, you come on out here." Bernadine confirmed.

"We Divas are here to support you." Cheri blurted out a few seconds later.

Ginger didn't budge. She wanted an answer that I couldn't give her.

"You have no idea, do you?" The corners of her mouth turned down after she asked the question. She propped herself up on the sink with her legs dangling. "There were a lot of people who don't like Doug, but who would want to kill him?"

I thought about the orders I got from the distributer. The beads come on a length of yarn to cushion them and keep them from breaking against each other. The ends were tied with very tight knots. Every time I cut them off, I think

I could make a really cool hat or knitted a sweater from all the yarn I was throwing away—if only I was a knitter.

"We can't talk about this here." I whispered. "What if the killer is here?"

"You gonna open up this door? Don't make me think of my ex-husband!" Bernadine yelled.

Ginger knew we wouldn't be able to discuss anything. Everyone was watching her, and her being locked in the bathroom with the owner of the shop Doug was found dead in would get the rumor-mill started.

When Ginger opened up the door, the Divas stumbled in as though they were pressed up against the door.

"Your husband told us he saw you come in here." Flora's phone was in its usual spot. "No, not you. I'll call you back." She flipped it shut.

I'd swear the space between her ear and shoulder had to be a cell charger, because the damn thing never ran out of battery life. Another reason not to have a cell phone—I was not going to be a slave to an electronic device.

The Divas and I filed out of the bathroom one by one.

Jim Rush stood in the corner of the kitchen with his butt up against the lazy susan. I cringed, knowing that Ginger keeps her cooking spices in there. Cooking spices and Jim Rush's butt were not a combination my taste buds could tolerate.

"Look at all this food." Cheri's eyes widened. She popped a couple of crackers covered with some sort of concoction into her mouth.

I have no idea where she puts all the food. Slender and young, her straight brown hair was pulled up in a high ponytail that hung past her shoulders, and blunt bangs framed her large brown eyes.

I put the veggie tray on the counter next to three trays that were identical to it.

One thing I didn't do was eat food from other peoples' kitchens I hadn't seen. I'd heard about people who let their animals walk on their counters or tables. What if the food they were preparing fell on the floor? Willow won't even eat off the floor.

Not Cheri. She didn't care where her next meal came from. I guess that's the way it is with college kids. Cheri reached for a finger sandwich and took a bite. Her eyes closed in delight.

When Cheri said she wanted to be a Diva, we asked her show us her divorce papers before she could join. One crazy night, during the summer between her high school graduation and first day of college, she went to Vegas and had a few too many cocktails with an Elvis impersonator. The next morning, she woke up with his wig on and a bald guy sleeping next to her.

Luckily, her mom was a divorce attorney, and with a quickie annulment, she was a divorcee.

Noah Druck walked into the kitchen. The Divas surrounded him and began to ask all sorts of questions, but he didn't pay them any attention. His eyes were focused on me.

He walked over to me and crossed his arms.

"I'm surprised to see you here under the circumstances." His voice was cold.

"What circumstances?" I asked. I could feel all the eyes in the room studying Noah and me.

Had the community already pegged me as the killer?

Noah turned, but stopped. "Just don't leave town." He tilted his head toward Jim and Ginger before walking out the back door.

The room went silent and now everyone was staring at me.

I decided that I'd been humiliated enough. I stormed out the front door and stomped down the street. Maybe I'd lose a couple more pounds from the steam I was blowing off.

I had to talk to Sean and fast. He had to have some answers to some questions I needed answered. He'd had mixed words with Doug on several occasions. Besides Marlene, Sean was also one of the last people to see Doug alive.

I didn't have to go very far to find him. When I reached the shop, I could see the sparkle from Marlene's white teeth chomping her gum and smiling at Sean as he leaned up against the counter—looking at her boobs, I'm sure.

Chapter Thirteen

"Hey, Holly." Sean had a playboy smile that could make a woman's heart melt.

I wanted to tell Marlene not to be fooled by his dashing good looks, that for some reason God graced him with, but I knew she was a diva and knew all too well what kind of guy he really was.

He was here for one of two reasons. Either he didn't have a job and next month's alimony was going to be late, or he was there to tell me how he'd taken a strand of beads from my shop and killed Doug with them.

Willow darted out of the back room to my side.

"What are you doing here?" I asked Sean as I bent down to pat Willow.

One pat was all she needed before she snorted her way back to the storage room to get far away from Marlene's heels.

It was hard not to stare at Sean and his shaggy blonde hair with natural highlights from working outside in the sun. That was another thing I hated about him. If I wanted those subtle streaks, I'd have to pay an arm and a leg for them, and his sketchy alimony payments wouldn't allow for that.

My eyes couldn't help themselves. They traveled up his tanned and nicely toned legs, followed the lines of his brown cargo shorts, and over the curves of his arms. His black t-shirt emphasized his tan. It was amazing to me that a man wanted to stay tan all year round. He was a carpenter, and he did a lot of outside work, but one of the Divas saw him leaving Tan Your Hide.

"I got your message and I need to talk to you too." The way his green eyes pierced my soul gave me chills. He sneezed.

"Bless you," I said, not really meaning it. It just came out automatically. "Are you getting sick?"

He sneezed again. "I don't think so." He rubbed his nose.

There were a couple of customers picking through the clearance bead section at the front of the shop. Marlene walked over to see if they had any questions, leaving me free to speak privately with Sean.

I crossed my arms to hide my stomach, and I noticed a disappointed look in his eyes. I couldn't press too hard on my midsection. I was a bit sore from my daily walks. It was good sore, so maybe the walks around the lake were doing some good. The small ache made me want to walk more.

He'd never approved of any type of elastic in my wardrobe, and when I'd hit double digits, his words were as dangerous as machine gun bullets.

"You didn't let anyone see what size that was when you bought it, did you?" He said once, and then he went down to The Livin' End and didn't return until the wee hours of the night.

"Doug Sloan was killed right there." I pointed to where his body was discovered just a few short days ago. I continued to separate the beads on the counter that Marlene had started. "You wouldn't know anything about that, would you?"

The customers scattered like flies when they heard me raise my voice.

"I'm going to get a cup of coffee." Marlene said, and grabbed her purse from behind the counter.

"Damn," I threw my hands in the air, "I can't afford to run people off."

I held my breath to hear what he had to say, hoping he would answer quickly, because I was never good at holding it for long.

"You saw me leave The Livin' End that night, right?" He leaned on his forearm across the counter.

I pushed his arm off the counter. There was no way I wanted to spend a Saturday cleaning the top of the glass because of Sean's arm fog. I hesitated before I answered. Making him sweat it out made me pleased as punch.

"Right?" He asked. There was a pleading tone in his voice.

"Are you talking about when Noah Druck came to question me about me being at The Livin' End because a little bird told him I was there?" I narrowed my eyes. "Or the fact you might've killed Doug Sloan right here in my shop?"

Sean looked down at his feet and took a few steps back.

The look was a dead give-away that he was the one who'd told Noah I was at The Livin' End that night. As much as I wanted to see Sean behind bars, I didn't think he was a killer or even had the intelligence to use a string of beads. Cracking Doug's head with a hammer was more his style, not anything to do with fashion.

"Oh." His usually bright smile was covered with tightly pressed lips.

"Did he tell you that Doug was strangled with a strand of beads just like these?"

I walked over to the hanging shelves and noticed the strand was missing. It was there yesterday. I quickly searched through the other hundreds of strands of hanging beads to see if the cat eyes had been misplaced, but they weren't there.

"What?" Sean stood behind me peering over my shoulder. "Gotta love the shelving."

"Did you take the strand of beads?" I had a handful of strands clutched in my fists, shaking them at his smug face. "Did you kill Doug Sloan? Did you try to frame me? "

One of the strands came unfastened and the beads fell and bounced all over the floor.

We both bent down to catch them at the same time and our heads smacked together.

"Ouch." Sean stood up rubbing his head. It was too late. The beads were lost in The Under. "No. I don't even know what a beaded eye looks like."

"Cat eye beads!" I screamed at the top of my lungs. "You're as dumb as a…"

"Enough, Holly." Nervously he ran his hands through his hair. "I didn't do it. Don't you believe me?"

Unbelievable. Did I believe him? There was a time that I trusted him, until I'd caught him in a few too many lies.

"Have you ever heard of the boy who cried wolf?" I glared at him, and walked over to the counter with Sean on my heels.

I knew he hadn't killed Doug. But who had?

"Looks like we're both suspects." He muttered, coming eye to eye with me, both hands planted on the counter. He turned his head as the bell above the shop door rang, signaling someone had come in.

"Hi, let me know if you need any help." I winced when I saw them.

The two ladies from this morning were back.

"The sign does say open." They both pointed to the door with the sign.

They liked to look at the beads and a thumb through some of the beading books. Whenever I asked them if I could help, they politely said no and went on their way without buying a thing.

I nodded. "Yes, we are now open."

I turned back to Sean. He was staring at the place on the floor where Doug's body had been.

"Well, you're the one who had a fight with him in public the night he was killed." I whispered through gritted teeth.

"Shhh." His neck craned, looking at the two women hovering over the charm selections. "I'm telling you, I didn't do it."

The plumper of the two women glanced over her glasses, making eye contact with me, and then quickly looked away. She tapped her friend on the arm and they made a beeline for the door.

"Thank you!" I shouted in a sarcastic tone. "This isn't the place or the time to talk about this. That's two sets of customers you ran off."

"You believe me don't you, Holly?" Sean asked.

"Depends." I said. "Give me your grandmother's chandelier."

He pulled back and stood as straight as a pin. His chest heaved with frustration.

"Never, Holly Harper!" Sean yelled, and then turned to leave. "I'd rot in jail before I'd give you that heirloom."

"Then you don't need me to get you off the hook. Get your dead grandmother to help you!" I screamed at the back of his head before he slammed the door.

I wasn't sure what the right time and place to discuss how the two of us are murder suspects would be, but it definitely wasn't right then. Even though I knew those two women weren't going to buy anything, I still wasn't happy he'd run them off with all his whispering.

I was beginning to regret not taking Jim up on his free surveillance installation. He'd said the camera was all I would have to pay for, but who'd steal from a bead shop? More importantly, who would want to pin a murder on me?

Chapter Fourteen

I didn't accomplish anything after Sean left. My mind was in no shape to bead, sort, or stock. I even sent Marlene home after she came back from getting her coffee. People shuffled in and out all day asking all sorts of questions about how to make a bracelet or earrings, but most of the banter was about the murder of Doug Sloan.

Marlene had called to say she wouldn't be able to make it to the Divas' meeting tonight, which put me in a bad spot, because she was the one who was supposed to be bringing the food. Luckily, shortly after her call, Ginger called to tell me she was coming and said she could bring some of the leftovers from earlier.

She didn't say a word about how the family was doing. She acted as though everything was okay and said she'd be there on time. That was a sure sign she wasn't doing well. Ginger was never on time. She was just like Elizabeth Taylor. She'd be fifteen minutes late to her own funeral.

When Cheri came home, she took Willow upstairs for a quick nap before the Divas arrived, which would be soon. They trickled in one by one.

"I heard about the fight." Flora mentioned with her cell phone stuck on her ear. "No, not you. I'm at my divorcee meeting. I'll call you back."

She snapped her cell shut just in time for it to ring in again.

Of course, she'd heard about the fight I'd had with Sean. If I were a betting woman, I'd say Marlene was on the phone with the Divas as soon as she walked out to get her coffee this morning. I'm sure it was all over Swanee by now.

Flora had perfect high cheekbones that any woman would crave and the ivory skin to match. She had to be one of those girls who never got a pimple, even during *that* time of the month. Her wavy light brown hair was enough to convince you that she just walked off the beach.

"I just can't believe it. No way, no how, do I believe you killed Doug." Bernadine sifted through the bead boxes, putting mismatched beads in their correct spot. "But Sean is a different story. Do you think that your lying, very good-looking ex-husband did it and is trying to set you up? You know he'd not only get all the jobs in town, but he could also stop paying alimony if you were in jail."

That was a quit a mouthful to digest. Of course, I had thought about it, but obviously all of Swanee thought about it too. Have they already convicted Sean?

"That's too easy." I got all our different projects out of the storage closet and put them on the tables.

I closed the shop so we could work on our projects and discuss what was going on in our lives, just like we had at meetings at the church. When I met Bernadine there, I thought she was so nosy, hanging around all the conversations. She was always going around the room collecting everyone's trash and cleaning up after them, but she wasn't really being nosy.

Bernadine had to be the neatest person in Swanee, right down to her appearance. Bernadine's marriage was like the ones you hear about where the couple wakes up one day and realize that they don't know each other.

He'd come out better off than Bernadine. She got the house on the lake across from my cottage, and he got their huge mansion in Ft. Meyers, Florida. There was still a bitter taste in Bernadine's mouth. After all, she had moved to Swanee for him.

He thought he wanted the small town life, while she wanted the beach and sand. When it came down to the end,

Bernadine was the one who ended up loving Swanee and all her new friends.

"Please don't sort the beads." I noticed Bernadine had moved onto the tiny seed beads that were virtually impossible to keep separated.

"Nah, I can do it until everyone else gets here." She knotted her long crimson hair in a bun so she could dig through the beads without hair in her face.

I wasn't going to bother trying reason with her. If she weren't sorting beads, she'd be in the office arranging the desk. My mind and heart didn't have the energy to argue. Plus, what she'd said about Sean was weighing heavily on my mind.

"Hello!" Ginger yelled as she came into the shop.

Cheri followed Ginger in with her backpack slung over one shoulder.

Willow ran straight over to them. Cheri took one of the foil trays out of Ginger's arms.

"You have to eat all this food before I gain ten more pounds," Ginger said. They sat the trays along the counter, which was the usual place we put food. Ginger took a bottle of wine out of her purse. "And this."

I drug my finger along my elastic waistband to remind me not to eat the cookies that were still wrapped up in the shop boxes. I was determined to lose this weight one way or another.

No matter how normal Ginger was trying to act, there was still a little uneasiness between us. I wasn't sure what to say, so it was was just easier to keep my mouth shut and let the other Divas do the talking.

Flora came back in, sweeping her hair behind her shoulders and giving Ginger a big hug.

"If you need anything, you let me know." She handed Ginger a card. "If you need a good lawyer, my ex might've been a bad husband, but he's a cutthroat lawyer. Right, Holly?"

I nodded, not sure what she wanted me to say. I barely knew the man. He only drew up the few papers that I needed to establish The Beaded Dragonfly.

"I told her we were all here for her. Just like we are here for everyone. Right, Holly?" Cheri raised her eyebrows, waiting for me to agree.

"Why is everyone right Hollying me?" I stopped and looked at them.

"What's this?" Bernadine was near the storage closet putting away some of the empty boxes I had left out while putting up the rest of the inventory.

She held a note in her hand, reading to herself.

"Holly." Her eyes grew big. Bernadine stood there with a blank expression, amazed and visibly shaken. "I think you are being framed for the murder of Doug Sloan."

Her hands shook as she held the note out for me to take. Ginger and the other Divas tripped over themselves to see what the note said.

I read the typewritten letter out loud, "Meet me on the pier by the lake or there will be blood on your hands. 10 p.m. tonight."

The note clung to my hands, like it was glued there. My feet felt heavy, and I stood there, more uncertain than ever.

"We need to call the police." Cheri grabbed the note.

Ginger looked over her shoulder as Cheri read it out loud.

"I understood it the first time." I reminded them I didn't need to hear it again.

I didn't want to hear about it anymore. Whoever it was wanted me to meet them by my cottage, and they had mentioned blood. I don't do well when blood is involved.

"Who was here today?" Ginger asked.

"Only a couple of customers, Marlene, and Sean."

"Marlene and Sean?" Bernadine sounded suspicious. "Where is Marlene tonight?"

"Don't be silly." I put the notion out of my head.

Marlene wouldn't hurt a fly, or at least I thought so. Granted, we didn't know much about her, but what I did know, I liked.

Bernadine tapped her watch with a bright red fingernail. "We've got fifteen minutes. We can all pile in my Suburban."

She grabbed the note from Cheri, which I wished they'd stop passing around because the police wouldn't be able to get any good prints off it.

"No." Flora ripped part of it out of Bernadine's grasp. "I think we should take it to the police."

"Great, you ripped it." Bernadine went into the office and came back with the tape dispenser.

"I think we should at least go see who it is." Ginger patted my arm. "I know you didn't have anything to do with Doug's murder. I'm not so sure about Sean or Marlene, but not you. Let's go see and then go to the police."

That was all the Divas needed to hear. We all piled into the Suburban like sorority girls going to a keg party. Even Willow snorted with excitement. Kinda laughing, kinda nervous…kinda scared.

Chapter Fifteen

"We can hide under the pier," Cheri yelled from the third seat.

I'd just walked around this lake with Bernadine last night, but the pier had never seemed scary to me—until now.

Some of the boards were broken, some had nails sticking out of them, and some just looked completely rotted. I wouldn't walk out onto it in broad daylight, much less hide under it in the dark.

"No…nope; I refuse to go hide under that pier." I folded my arms in protest.

The note was obviously left for me, and I didn't plan to be the next victim. We were only there to find out who had left the note, and then we were planning to go straight to Noah.

"Fine." Flora also yelled from the third row of seats. "We'll park at your house and hide in the woods."

That was the best idea Flora had in a long time. The woods were between my cottage and the lake. It would be the perfect place to hide.

Moonlight reflected off the dark surface of the water whenever it wasn't hidden behind a passing cloud. We could see Bernadine's solar powered lights that ran from her house down to her boat dock twinkling across the lake.

"Tiptoe and keep quiet," I admonished everyone before we got out of the car. "Now, we aren't going to get too close. We just need to get close enough to see who it is."

I put Willow in the house and quickly pulled on my rain boots. I'd been through those woods many times and they could make a mess of your shoes in a hurry.

The Divas were about as quiet as a bull in a china shop. None of them must have ever played Clue or Spy before.

"Oh, Yuck!" Flora lifted up a foot to examine her shoe.

A glop of muck and leaves hung from the high heel.

"Shh." Did I really need to remind them that my life was on the line?

I held my hand out to quiet them. I could hear twigs breaking in the distance. We stopped dead in our tracks. A flashlight was flickering near the pier. We needed to get closer, and we needed to get there fast. It was already after ten, and I desperately wanted to see who was threatening me.

We saw three shadowy figures standing close to the pier that seemed to be in a heated discussion—make that a shouting match.

Like in a cheerleading pyramid, I was on top of the other Divas trying to hear what they were saying. I needed to know if they were waiting for me. I was pretty sure they thought I wouldn't show up.

The wind started up a little more, and the trees began to sway more violently.

"Who is that?" Bernadine pulled her glasses out of her pocket and put them on. "It sorta looks like..."

Suddenly, the moon came out from behind a cloud and lit up the lakeshore as bright as day.

"No." Flora gasped in disbelief, as one of the shadows stepped into the moonlight.

The silence of our little group was absolute as we watched full-figured Marlene stomp back to her car, leaving the two others angrily screaming at her from the dock.

"Marlene?" Ginger looked over at me with a questioning look in her eyes.

Sure, there were some things about Marlene that we didn't know. Like how both her husbands had died, or where she was from, or if she'd ever had a job other than the part-time one I'd given her at the shop. Okay, there was a lot of stuff we didn't know about her, but she seemed to fit in with everyone. Everyone that is, except for Ginger. Even though Ginger was my best friend, that wouldn't Marlene any reason to leave a threatening note for me or frame me for murder.

Cheri grabbed hold of my shirt and pulled me back out of view. The other two women at the dock waddled back to their car.

"I know them," I whispered to the Divas when Marlene's headlights passed over them.

Flora, Ginger, Cheri, and Bernadine asked in unison, "Who are they?"

Cheri's eyes grew wide and her mouth formed an O as her jean jacket pocket started singing *Don't Be Cruel*.

"Shhh!" The rest of us didn't realize how loud we were being.

"Who's there?" One of the two women shouted from the car and pointed the flashlight into the woods. "Who's there?"

Instantly, we took off running. I had a sharp pain in my side from being out of shape. I used to be able to run that distance with no problem, but I couldn't seem to catch my breath. I didn't look back until we were halfway to the cottage. There were branches breaking underfoot behind me.

Flora emerged from the trees with her heels under her arm. Bernadine was right behind her and looked like a modern day version of a Greek goddess with leaves sticking out from her hair. They were followed by a tangled mass of scarves flowing in the wind, and I knew Ginger had to be in there somewhere. Bringing up the rear was the ever-so-cool Cheri with her beret perched on her head like a bird's nest.

" Holly, I'm so sorry." Cheri bent down trying to catch her breath. "I totally forgot my phone was on."

"Who were those women and why was Marlene with them?" Flora asked.

"Did Marlene write that note?" Bernadine asked, pushing Cheri's hair back up in her barrette. She had apparently forgotten we were on a stakeout and not on a runway.

I put my finger to my lips and motioned for them to follow me. I didn't hear any sounds of movement, and was sure the women couldn't have caught up to us. I wasn't sure if the coast was clear, but we made it into the cottage and plopped down on the couches without turning any lights on.

I parted the curtain just as a pair of headlights passed by, and I figured it was the two women leaving. I flipped on the light and instantly began screaming along with the other Divas.

"Really? This is what the oh-so-great divorced Divas do at their meetings?" Sean was sitting at the kitchen table with a smug look on his face.

"No, don't kill us!" Bernadine grabbed Flora whose phone was pressed up against her ear. "Call 911, Flora."

"I'm not going to kill anyone." Sean laughed.

"Why should we believe you?" Ginger asked and hid behind Bernadine who was hiding behind Cheri. Cheri was barely visible behind Flora, but I knew she had her keys in her fist.

"Did you kill my brother?" Ginger squeaked out her question.

"Hang up the phone." I said to Flora and then turned back to Sean. "Why are you here and sitting in the dark?"

The Divas were piled on top of each other like Keystone cops and standing still as posts. There wasn't a single twitch. This was the first time I've seen the Divas go more than one second without saying a word.

"Girls, he hasn't killed anyone, and he isn't going to tonight. Right?" I said and looked for confirmation from Sean.

"Right. I just needed to talk to Holly, and I saw the suburban outside. I didn't know who it belonged to, so I let myself in and waited in the dark." He never took his eyes off the Divas. "I didn't want someone calling the police if they noticed the lights were on and Holly's bug wasn't here."

He did have a point. If I would've come home and saw that my lights were on, I would've driven right back into town to the police station. Maybe I should get a cell phone.

"Where is your car?" Cheri asked.

Flora nodded her head like a bobbing buoy, "Yeah, good point. Where is it?" She pointed her slender finger with the big diamond from her ex-husband in his direction.

"I parked it up the hill, off the road." He got up and the Divas stepped back, still holding onto each other. "Listen, I'm outta here. Call me tomorrow so we can talk."

I put my hand up. Doug's murder and our sneaking around had stirred up a little too much excitement for everyone.

"You should stay. They were leaving anyway." My eyebrows lifted and I made a zipper motion across my lips. "We can talk tomorrow."

"What about Marlene?" Ginger whispered to me on the way out.

"I'll be right back." I told Sean and followed them out to Bernadine's truck.

The night was black as coal, and there was a new chill in the air. Soon, the night fog would be rolling in and it would be nearly impossible to drive in. Sean and I could talk, and I'd have Bernadine drive me to the shop in the morning before her yoga class.

"Don't say a word to anyone about what we saw here tonight." I had to sort through what I knew about Marlene and try to piece some things together.

"I knew Marlene was no good from the moment I set eyes on her. I bet she offed my brother too," Ginger said, looking angry.

"Uh-huh." The divas all agreed with Ginger.

It was no secret that Marlene wanted Doug any way she could get him. But did she really want him dead?

They didn't have to say it, but I know they were curious about why Sean, who left a very bitter taste in my mouth, was making himself all too comfortable in the cottage.

I didn't stay to watch them pull out. I was freaked out enough and wanted that night to be over. Sean was sitting on the couch with Willow curled up next to him, snoring. She didn't mind all the ruckus as long as she could sleep.

"What were you *divorcees* up too?" He drug out the word he secretly hated.

When we were going through the divorce, he'd never say it. He thought "split-up" sounded better—better for his lying, cheating heart.

"It's really none of your business." I said. "How did you get in here?"

He flipped my spare key at me. "Pig's mouth."

Damn, I forgot that I'd had to call him from the shop a few weeks ago and asked him to let Willow out. She was recovering from a bellyache, and taking care of a sick pig was just as bad as taking care of a sick kid.

"Why are you here, Sean?" I opened the door, went outside, and put the key back in the ornamental concrete pig's mouth. I was going to have to find a new hiding spot, but this was not the night for it.

"So, are you trying to frame me, Hol?" He asked.

I hated when he used that shortened version of my name. Especially when the lighting in the cottage was making his green eyes sparkle more than usual.

"Well?" He asked again. "Are you?"

Frame him?

"You really think I'd be stupid enough to kill someone in my own shop, using my own inventory? And you don't have the right to call me Hol anymore." I rolled my eyes at his stupidity. "Now, you, on the other hand, have many reasons to have killed him in *my* shop with *my* beads."

"Why is that?" He stood up and crossed his arms.

I rubbed my waistband again. Every time he looked at me, I felt him judging my appearance.

"You weren't getting any jobs that weren't clean-ups from Doug's messes. If he was out of the picture, you'd get all the jobs." I stormed over and stood nose to nose with him. "Second, if I was in jail, you wouldn't have to pay alimony."

He threw his head back and laughed hysterically.

"Why is it that you never take me seriously? You never did when we were married, and now that we're both suspects, you think it's a big joke." I poked him in the chest. "Listen. We are all we got, whether we like it or not."

"You've watched too many episodes of this." He picked up a Veronica Mars DVD case off the top of the TV. "I think I'll leave it to the police."

I nearly jumped out of my skin when the phone rang. I checked the clock. It was after eleven and no one ever called that late.

"Who could that be?" Sean peeked out the window like someone was watching us.

Chills washed over me and I began to shiver.

Letting out a little moan, I cautiously answered the phone in a soft tone, "Hello?"

"Oh my God! Someone has destroyed the shop!" Cheri screamed through the phone, sounding panicked.

I stood speechless for a moment, replaying what I'd heard in my head.

"Hello? Holly?"

Sheer fright swept over me. There was definitely someone after me. So much for a relaxing night after such a crazy day.

Chapter Sixteen

"Do you know who could've done this?" Noah asked.

I had called the police on the way over. I'd need a report to file an insurance claim if something was missing or damaged or dead. Just by luck, Noah was on duty.

"Did you do this?" Noah asked me and then turned to Sean.

I was starting to become annoyed with his accusations.

"Yeah, Noah. I took everything I've worked to create and just decided to trash the place." I gestured around the shop.

Sean let out a loud sigh and rolled his eyes. That might've been the first time he and Noah had come face to face since the fight that ended their friendship. I never found out what the fight was about. I made a mental note to ask Sean about it.

It wasn't as bad as Cheri had made it out to sound. The front window was busted out and the tables and chairs had been flipped over. They obviously didn't want to do more than cause me a headache, because all the beads were left hanging and in the bead bins.

"It just looks suspicious, you know." He wrote away on the pad of paper like he was really taking notes.

That damn notepad. I secretly wished I could take a look at it.

He glanced up quickly and then looked back down. "To try and throw me off the trail. We find a dead body, and then someone breaks in. It makes it look like you're trying to clear yourself."

"When do you think you'll have the report? I'll need it to send to my insurance company," I said.

I wasn't going to let his accusations bother me. The awning over the shop's broken window was flapping in the wind, and I wrapped my arms around my body to shield it from the cold night air.

"It'll be ready tomorrow." Noah continued to write whatever it was he always wrote on his little pad. "Come by the station around noon."

Glass crunched under his black shoes as he left. He didn't bother stepping around it like any normal person would've done. I shook my head and wondered if there was any inventory missing. Of course, this would happen the one time I didn't check the items off the packaging slip.

"Dang," I muttered as I walked back to the office, hoping Marlene had left the slip sitting on the desk.

I barely caught myself as I tumbled over something.

"You okay?" Cheri asked me.

Sean was outside, sweeping the glass off the stoop.

I flipped on the office light, praying that I didn't just kick another dead body. Shards of glass glistened all over the desk. I picked up the brick I had tripped over and removed the note that was attached by a rubber band.

"Yes." I hesitated, wondering if I should tell them about this note. I yelled back, "I'm fine. Just a lot of glass."

I shut the office door and flattened the note out. If Marlene and the two women had something to do with Doug's murder and were trying to frame me for it, I wanted to know why. Doing it on my own might be the only way to clear Sean and me.

I read the note slowly, making sure I didn't miss anything. "I want the bead. What you did tonight only made matters worse." What bead?

I folded the note up and slipped it into my back pocket. I tugged my elastic up on my jeans and grabbed the extra broom from the storage closet. This was not going to make me close the shop. I was going to remain open no matter what. I didn't have a choice.

"I went ahead and put up some really strong plastic across the window." Sean pointed to the front of the shop.

Thank God, he was still at my house and drove his work truck. He always carried the craziest stuff in that truck. "Never know when you're going to need something," he'd say. And he was right tonight.

"Great. The office window has a little hole too. Do you think you can put some of the plastic on it?" I asked.

I was careful not to look at him. He was always able to read me and I didn't want to have to lie about the brick and the note. Marlene had been my friend from the time she joined the Divas and I didn't want to believe she had something to do with this.

"Too bad you don't have a security camera," Sean said.

"Yeah, too bad."

Maybe it was time I invested in a little more security. Not only for the shop, but also for myself. I admit if someone came up behind me, they'd be able to take me down. Granted, with my extra pounds I could possibly hurt them by falling on them, but I'd much rather be able to protect myself.

"Cheri, are you still taking that karate class at school?" I held the dustpan while she swept the broken glass into it.

"It's not karate. It's self defense," she corrected.

Karate, self defense, it's all the same when you want to do damage to someone.

"Are you interested in coming? We'd love to have you," she said and looked up.

I thought for a second about all the college kids in there and then me. I laughed.

"Can you imagine me in a self defense class when I can't even save myself from a few doughnuts?" I pulled on the elastic waistband, let go, and let it smack my pooch.

"As a matter of fact, I've really toned up since taking it. We do more than just defense moves. We start out with all sorts of muscle building exercises," Cheri said, and started doing some of the exercises involving all sorts of squat sequences.

I definitely needed some training in case my life really was in danger, but I had to say, losing weight at this point was pretty important too.

With Sean out of the way, I'd be able to discuss everything going on with Cheri and possibly talk a little more about the self-defense class.

"So, do you think the two women at the lake tonight had anything to do with this?" Cheri asked.

Slivers of glass were everywhere. Even *The Under* was glistening, and there was not a chance I was going to deal with that tonight.

"Yes." I pulled the note out of my back pocket and waited while Cheri read it.

Her eyebrows rose and fell with every word. She pulled the beret off her head. Her long dark hair flowed down to her shoulders.

She stomped around in a circle like a child. "No way! It has to be Marlene. What did you do to her?"

That was my first question, but the more I thought about it, the more I realized I'd done nothing but be her friend.

"Here's the deal. I don't want any of the Divas to know, especially Ginger. She was too much on her plate as it is."

Plus, I don't think Ginger really believes that Sean it is innocent. Yes, I've painted him as a bad, bad man to the Divas and he was—to me---but I know he isn't a killer.

I let Cheri in on a few of the details about the two plump women who had come into the shop a few times when I'd been there alone. Although, the last time was when Sean was there. I told her how they never buy anything or ask any questions. They just walk around and stare or try to peek in the back of the shop where the office and storage is.

"Plus, Marlene has access to all the beads; what bead is the note referring to?" Cheri glanced around.

"I don't have any expensive beads."

I did recall a time when Marlene wanted me to get these rondell beads that have real crystal instead of glass, but they were too expensive. Is that enough to make her mad at me, kill Doug, and then frame me?

She'd been trying to get her claws into Doug for a long time, and on several occasions, he'd turned her down. Was she just killing two birds with one stone?

"Has Marlene ever shared anything with you about her past?" I asked Cheri, looking for any clue.

"Nothing she hasn't shared with the Divas." Cheri took the last pan of broken glass and dumped it in the trash.

"I'm still going to have her work here and see if there's anything out of the ordinary." I checked the back door and made sure it was locked. "I still want to host the divorcee group next weekend"

"I have an idea," Cheri said. "We can play a game about our ex's and whoever wins gets a fabulous prize. But what could we use as the prize that won't be too expensive?"

"I can give a free private beading class of the winner's choice. They'd get everything for free."

Who wouldn't want that? Especially Marlene. The only reason she helped stock was so she could get free things.

Chapter Seventeen

I wasn't sure, but it seemed like ever since Doug's murder, there were more customers than ever. I was barely able to keep up. I was seeing new faces all the time, and some who had never picked up a bead in their lives. Going back to the basics made me remember how much I love to string the single, simple glass bead.

Sometimes I get too caught up in beading new and complex designs, but that week brought me back to the basics. Still, every time I walked over Doug's dead body spot, I shivered at the thought that someone hated me enough to frame me for murder.

Noah Druck was no closer to finding the killer than I was. He still came around with that damn notepad and pencil I wanted to grab and break in half.

Every night after work, Bernadine and I met at the pier and walked around the edge of the lake. It must have been working, because the waistband indentions weren't as deep as they were at the beginning of the week.

That day, I was meeting with Margaret and her mom to try to get some final designs on her bridesmaids' accessories.

Throughout the week, I had been putting together a variety of designs that included different color schemes for Margaret to pick from and to give her an idea of what I was thinking would work.

They were going to arrive at the shop any minute.

"Don't forget about tonight." Cheri popped her head in after she got home from her classes to remind me of my first self-defense class."

"Don't worry. I'll be there." Whether or not I wanted to go, I'd made a commitment and I was sticking to it.

One by one, I carefully carried out the designs for Margaret McGee on bead boards from the storage room. None of the necklaces were strung because she hadn't actually requested a certain style. This would also allow Margaret to switch out beads she didn't like.

The crystal antique, pink Swarovski element with the diamond rondelles were by far my favorite pick if Margaret was going for a soft, romantic look. The pink was very light, almost clear. When the sun hit them, they glistened. From what I remember, Margaret was having an outside wedding, making that necklace a perfect choice.

The two-toned Czech glass bead design was on the other end of the spectrum. The dark aurora borealis beads are edgy and eye catching. The brown seed-beads between each Czech really screamed for attention.

I had also created a few other designs that I considered "safe." Ultimately, it was Margaret's decision and I hope she decided to hire me.

I had been planning for this consultation for days and wanted to make it hard to leave without Margaret signing a contract. I even bought champagne and tea cookies to set a bridal mood.

When Margaret walked in, I handed her a fluke of bubbly, and offered her a couple of cookies. She was clearly pleased. I wanted to give Margaret an experience that would make her want to recommend The Beaded Dragonfly to her single, rich friends.

I would have done about anything right then to keep her business so I could gain more.

She walked up and down, looking at the designs I had laid out for her. I gave her a brief overview of the different designs. She spent a lot of time looking at the white lotus pearl.

"What if we did this pearl with the pink four-millimeter pink Swarovski crystal between them?" She held a few of the beads in her hand to show me her idea. "And one of these on each side."

I looked into the palm of her hand. Lotus pearl, two-millimeter sterling silver ball, four-millimeter pink Swarovski crystal, two-millimeter sterling silver ball, and Lotus pearl. It was a very pretty combination.

She laid the design out on one of the bead boards and grabbed a strand of pearls. She looked in the mirror that was hanging on the wall and draped the strand around her neck. Her long, brown hair cascaded down and made the pearls look elegant against her olive skin.

"I'm going to wear my hair down." She turned, looking at herself at all angels in the mirror. "My dress is strapless with a pink undertone."

Margaret McGee was going to be one beautiful bride with or without one of my designs.

"Stunning." I stood behind her, looking into the mirror at her image. "You look really beautiful in pearls."

I was so glad that at the last moment, I had come up with a design with pearls. Most of the time, I stay away from them because I love color.

Margaret smiled. She could've been a model in a teeth-whitening commercial, her teeth were *that* white.

"Well?" I held my breath. My business really depended on landing this project.

"Momma is going to be so happy that I've decided to go with the pearl design." She went back to the table where she laid out the design for her mother. "I want the one we designed for me, and the one you designed for the bridesmaids."

"Great choice, Margaret." I got a sales slip and a piece of paper, and I sat down at the table.

Quickly, I drew up the matching earrings and bracelet that would go with each bridesmaid so she could have a visual.

"I'm going to need each bridesmaid's wrist size." I explained to her that each bracelet was designed to fit, but the necklaces would be the standard sixteen inches in length.

I let out a sigh of relief when Margaret finally signed the contract, realizing that my dream was coming true.

Now, all I had to do was prove my innocence in Doug's murder, and if I could, Sean's innocence too.

Chapter Eighteen

"Beaded Dragonfly." I said as I answered the phone, hoping it was a call asking about the shop's hours of operation and not a beading question, becauseI didn't have much time to get across town to the Moose Lodge for my first self-defense class.

Most of the time, people call and ask all sorts of questions about beads they've seen on other people, but they don't know the names and begin describing them to me as "round, glass, pretty." Those adjectives describe most of the beads in my shop.

Regardless, I've wasted a lot of time trying to figure out which beads they are talking about over the phone, because they almost always end up coming into the shop to figure it out anyway.

"Holly." The voice was low and raspy.

For a split-second, I wondered if this was the murderer. They were finally getting in touch with me to tell me why they killed Doug in my shop. Or worse…that I was next.

"Holly, you there?" The voice sounded vaguely familiar.

"Umm…yes." I was cautious.

"Thank, God. I need you now." Sadie was no longer disguising her voice. "I know he is cheating on me now. I need you to meet me at this bar and go in to see if he's with a girl."

"Sadie, where are you?" I checked the clock on the wall. I had a little over an hour until my self-defense class.

Week, week, week. Willow's big black eyes stared up at me. She was starving. I bent down and patted her on the head. *Humph*, she fell to the ground and rolled over for a good belly scratch.

"I'm at The Livin' End." She was angry. "I followed him here. You said you'd help."

"And how exactly do you expect me to help?" I walked through the shop, finishing the nightly duties, and shutting off the lights.

"I have a picture of him. You can look at it and then go into the bar to see if you see him with a girl." Sadie sniffed into the phone.

I'm a sucker for a crying woman, especially one that was being cheated on.

"Fine. I have to take Willow home and then I will be there."

"Hurry, Holly," She said. "If he walks out with another woman, I just might kill him."

"Don't do that. The last thing we need in Swanee is another murder."

I clipped on Willow's leash, locked the shop door and we got in the car. Sadie's words replayed in my head and I pushed the accelerator down a little more, making my VW go faster.

Luckily, Swanee wasn't that big and I got Willow home, fed, and put to bed. Then I grabbed my yoga pants for defense class. I wasn't going to have time to change at home since I was headed to The Livin' End. I'd have to change at the Moose Lodge.

I pulled into bar's parking lot and parked next to Sadie. She was sitting on the hood of her car as if she was waiting to pounce on her prey.

"Get in the car." I shooed her to her door. "No self-respecting, cheated on woman acts like this."

She jumped around and snapped her fingers. "So you do think he's cheating."

"Give me the picture and get in the car." I demanded.

I had to pee, so it was a good excuse to go in.

I took a long look at the picture of Sadie's cheating husband. I did a double take when I noticed he was sporting a purple Mohawk. If he still had that hairdo, he sure wouldn't be hard to find. I glanced around the smoky bar.

The jukebox was blaring, but the drunks bellied up to the bar were louder. The line to the women's bathroom was down the hall and around the corner of the bar. I planted my feet in line, determined not to let any drunken woman cut in front of me, which almost always happened when I was there.

"I don't remember seeing anyone fighting that night." The bartender yelled from behind the bar.

Without looking to see who he was talking to, I kept my head down.

"Listen, we don't want any trouble here. We're just trying to figure out who killed Doug Stone." Noah said from the other side of the bar.

I tilted my head slightly to make sure it was him. He and another Swanee officer were writing away on their little notepads.

I rolled my eyes. I'd give anything to see read that thing Noah was always writing in.

At least he was here following up and not just going around accusing people without evidence.

"If I knew something. I'd have told you." The bartender pulled the tap and filled a frosty mug with the cheap beer. "If I remember something, I'll call you."

Noah and the other officers nodded and walked out.

Finally, I got to the bathroom, and when I was finished, I walked through the entire bar. Definitely no purple Mohawks. As a matter of fact, there wasn't a mohawk in sight.

Sadie was back out on the hood of her car. She threw her hands in the air. "What took you so long?"

"I had to pee. But he wasn't in there." I said, and looked at the picture one last time before I gave it back to her.

I wanted to make sure I got all the details so I could tell the Divorced Divas about this. Not that they'd be surprised that Sadie had asked me to spy, but that her husband has a purple Mohawk.

Chapter Nineteen

I parked my car next to a light pole. That was something I'd learned from the defenseforyou.com website when deciding whether or not to go through with this class. Nothing had happened in the past week to make me feel like someone was watching me, making me more and more suspicious of Marlene.

My curiosity was really piqued when she called saying she wouldn't be able to help me this week. It would be the first time she hadn't stepped foot in the shop on a day we were open in six months. I made a mental note to stop in and check on Agnes to make sure nothing had happened to her.

The class was in the old Moose Lodge on the outskirts of town.

There were only a few people attending. I looked around for Cheri.

"Up here," Cheri said, and motioned for me to come up front.

I shook my head vigorously, but she continued to wave me up. I'd much rather be in the back when I fall on my face.

"Psychological confidence/strength is half the battle," the young buff instructor stated.

Of course that's easy, I wanted to say to him, when you look like you.

"Using this is the other half." He used his hands as wands to indicate our bodies.

I glared at Cheri. This seemed a waste of time. I looked down at my new yoga pants I had bought. There were a few extra lumps around my midsection; maybe a jazzercise class would've been better.

"I am going to teach *you*," He pointed straight at me and continued, "how to use your body as a weapon."

I couldn't help but smile as the crowd, well—few people, cheered him on. He was definitely charming.

"Isn't he great?" Cheri beamed. "He's just your type."

Instantly, I realized why I was there. Cheri had been trying to set us up.

"Oh, no you don't." I pointed at her. "I don't need a date."

There was nothing worse than being set up while you're wearing yoga pants.

"Just give him a chance." Cheri's eyes were begging me. "You do need a date."

I watched Mr. Macho give us the first piece of advice. He pointed to his head. "Use your brain. When you leave your car, use your keys."

He demonstrated how to hold our keys with the sharp edges sticking out and stabbed the air. If someone could use a string of cat eye beads to kill Doug, they'd surely be able to take my keys from my trembling hand.

Mancho Man's ideas weren't making me think he was so brainy. He did a couple demonstrations with a few of the other eager clients, but I watched with skepticism. Cheri, on the other hand, was practicing by mimicking every move he did on her air dummy.

"You have to participate." She jabbed her keys toward me. "I told him about the Doug thingy."

Great. I'd become known as the Doug thingy.

"Come on, Holly." Mancho Man executed a couple of quick jabs, causing me to flinch.

"Try it." He did the move again, trying to coax me.

I half-heartedly flung my hand out in the air.

As quick as lightening, and before I knew it, he had his hands around me.

"Use your brain." He pointed to my head. "Tight fist around the keys. An intruder could smack those keys right out of your loose hand."

He smacked my hand to cause me to tighten my grip.

"Yep. Good." He gave me a thumbs-up and moved on.

Annoyed, I did a few more air jabs to make Cheri happy.

When class was over, I wanted to get out of there as quickly as possible. I was embarrassed, and I was never coming back.

"Holly?" Mancho Man yelled.

I almost made it out the door. I put my keys in the palm of my hand like a weapon. I turned around to find him walking toward me. His biceps seemed a little more flexed than they should be as he took the towel and rubbed it across his forehead.

I'm not sure what class he was in, but there wasn't a single bead of sweat on me. Still, I couldn't look away from his deep green eyes. There was something there, telling me to wait.

"Cheri told me about why you were coming." There was the look of sympathy I'd been getting all week. "I really do think you need to learn how to defend yourself."

I sucked my stomach in and stood a little taller when he reached out and touch my arm. Oh, how I hoped it didn't feel flabby to him.

"I told Cheri I'd be more than happy to come to the Divas weekly meeting to give a lesson on a different move each week," he said.

How could she? I noticed Cheri had made a beeline out to her car and zoomed off before I could say anything to her.

The Divas meetings were for ranting *about* men, not inviting them. They were also for beading, eating, and maybe a little bit of gossip too.

"Let me get back with you on that." I turned back to my car. I didn't kill Doug, but I might kill Cheri.

How stupid. The keys cut into the palm of my hand from making my fist a little tighter. They would make a good weapon for at least one jab. I punched the air, and a little wave of confidence shot through me. Maybe there was something to this self-defense stuff.

At least I'd parked near the light. I slid my key in the lock. I'd give it another chance. Besides, no one else was going to defend me.

Chapter Twenty

"You can't bring a pig into the police station." Noah Druck tried to shoo Willow out of the old station by using his hand that was holding a doughnut, but Willow tripped him up by smelling his shoes.

A snort came out, and Noah dropped his donut. Willow snatched it up and downed it in one gulp.

"Get her out of here." Noah pointed to the door. "All our evidence will be eaten up if she stays in here."

"You didn't need that doughnut anyway." I didn't pay attention to Noah Druck's order. "Did you want to see me or not?"

The other officers snickered. They'd already gotten a good dose of Willow while taking all those fingerprints, and weren't going to mess with her.

"Hi, Jim." I wasn't sure if I should smile or not. "How's Ginger doing? I really need to call her."

It was still uncomfortable. Even if she didn't suspect me of killing her brother, she didn't extend that to my ex-husband.

Jim was standing on the step stool adjusting some video cameras in the corner near the door. He pulled the screwdriver away and gave me a half-hearted smile.

"It's hard. Doug was a pain in her ass, and mine too for that matter, but he was a good guy." Jim was always getting Doug out of trouble for Ginger.

They were always together, sort of like brothers.

"I heard about the shop getting broken into." Jim said, and shook his head. "I wish we knew what was going on around here."

I glared at Noah. No one was supposed to know about the break-in.

"For goodness sakes, Holly, he works around here." Noah said, trying to smooth things over. He took a seat in the chair behind his desk.

"You should think about installing a couple of cameras." Jim stepped off the stool. "With the way things are going around town, I'm getting calls left and right."

He was right. I'd been blowing him off ever since I opened the shop. There hadn't been a need for security cameras in a town like Swanee. Until now.

"I'll think about it." I said, and held up the note from Noah Druck I had found on my door. "You stopped by?"

Noah summoned me over to his desk.

"Where were you last night?" He asked, and pulled out that damn notebook from his shirt pocket.

Should I answer quickly, or take time to think about it? Which one made me look worse? If I answered too quickly, it might make me look nervous. If I took some time, it might make me look like I was hiding something.

"Are you accusing me of something?" I asked and sat down in the chair in front of his desk. My shoulders sagged and I swallowed hard.

"No, but I came by the shop and your house. You're generally at one or the other." He tapped the notebook with his pen.

"Why do you need to know?" This cat and mouse game was getting very interesting.

"Have you forgotten there was a dead man found in your shop?" He began to tap harder. I could see he was making indentions on the small pad.

"I think you need to take this." The other officer interrupted us, held out the phone. "It's important."

Noah motioned for me to stay, as though I was going to jump up and escape. The other officer gave me a look.

I'm not sure what kind of look, but I knew it wasn't a good one.

Noah came back to the desk and hovered over me. "Exactly where were you last night?"

I would've given him a smart-ass answer, but he didn't look like he was playing around.

"I was at a new defense class last night. I thought if someone is after me, I'd better learn how to defend myself." I chopped the arm of the chair.

"When was the last time you saw Sean?" He sat back down in his chair.

Did they really have sufficient evidence to arrest Sean? He'd been showing up at the shop, and even at the house.

Last night when I got home, Willow was going crazy like she does when he's around. He left a message on my answering machine, but the machine was so old that the tape bunched up, causing the thing to jam, and all I got was something about, "Marlene," before it cut off.

This morning, Willow stopped to smell a footprint in the mud. The print did look like the bottom of one of Sean's work boots, the only boots he ever buys. He must've stopped by.

"I mean it. When was the last time you saw him?" Noah's sounded serious.

I drew back, putting some distance between us. "I don't know. I guess the night the shop was broken into. Why?"

Noah stepped back and straightened up. "It appears Sean didn't make it over to Agnes Pearl's this morning to finish the job Doug started. He told her he would be there first thing. When she sent Marlene to his house, his truck was gone."

One thing was for sure, when Sean told you he was going to be there, he would be there.

The answering machine could have the answer. The machine had seen better days. Hell, I wasn't sure if they even made those anymore. Flora was always getting on me about a new phone with caller ID and a built-in answering service.

"Is there something you need to tell me?" Noah asked. "You seem like you just thought of something."

"Nope." I shook my head.

Yes, I was thinking of something. Why did Sean stop by my house? What did he say about Marlene? And where

was he? Sean definitely was making himself seem guilty.
But I knew better.

I had to find Sean and get some answers.

"Come on, Willow." I stood up and made eye contact
with Noah.

"Don't leave town." His face was stern, almost
accusing.

I grabbed my things, and forgot about the note he had
left on my door. I drug Willow snorting along the floor.
She was pulling the opposite direction of me, probably
trying to get at morsel of food on the floor.

In light of Sean missing, whatever Noah wanted to talk
to me about last night had now been put on the back burner.
He needed to find Sean, and I needed to find Sean.

This wasn't good on so many levels. I checked the date
on my watch. I had less than a week to figure this out. My
rent was due, and I needed my alimony.

Chapter Twenty-one

Before I headed over to Agnes Pearl's house, I decided to make a quick stop in the parking lot of Sloan's Hardware. It was the location of the last remaining phone booth in town.

I counted out fifty cents from the coins in my car's ashtray and plunked them into the old pay phone.

"Sean, where are you? Noah said that you were going to Agnes' house to finish up some work." I inhaled deeply. This was not like him. "You need to call me ASAP."

I hung up the receiver and jumped as someone placed a hand on my shoulder.

"Why so jumpy?" Ginger stood behind me. "You really need a cell phone. I leave this pay phone up just for you because you are the only one who still uses it."

"Oh, Ginger. I'm so worried." I hugged my friend for comfort. Doug was dead and now Sean was missing. My world was turning upside down, just when I was getting it back on track. "Sean is missing. Or at least he doesn't want to be found."

Ginger bit her lip like she did when she doesn't want to talk.

"What?" I took her by the shoulder. "Now is not the time to keep something from me."

She shuffled her shoe through loose pieces of gravel on the pavement.

"Tell me, Ginger." I pleaded.

"It's just that Sean is making himself look very suspicious." Ginger folded her arms. "I didn't think he could do something like this, but it doesn't look good. The police are going to name him a suspect, and…"

I looked into her eyes when she stopped.

"And what?" I waited in anticipation.

"They are going to name a couple more suspects," she said. "And I want you to know that I know you didn't do it."

"Me? They are going to name me?" My heart stopped. "What in the world did I have against your brother?"

"I know. It's ridiculous, but Noah got an anonymous tip saying you had told someone that if Doug wasn't around, Sean could get the work around town and pay his alimony on time." Ginger bit her lip again.

I racked my brain to remember if I said it, but I couldn't think clearly. It might've been a true statement, but I couldn't recall saying it.

"I've got to go." I didn't wait for Ginger to respond. I jumped into my car.

I had to get to Agnes Pearl's.

Pulling up to Agnes' gingerbread mansion brought back incredible childhood memories. The sprawling twenty acres wasn't nearly enough land for Agnes Pearl's bigger than life world. It blew my mind the first time I'd seen it. Even as a kid, I looked around every corner just for a peek of Agnes.

"Who's there?" Agnes called out after I tapped on the wooden screen door.

There it was—the red feather silhouette flapping on top of her head as her shadow on the wall came closer to the door.

"It's me, Holly Harper." I called into the screen.

I was filled with giddiness as the feather silhouette fluttered through the dimly lit foyer. The sunlight danced through the lead-glass windows in her foyer, giving it a kaleidoscopic effect. Agnes appeared with her purple turban a little cockeyed on top of her head. The hot pink jewel that kept the feather in place was in desperate need of a little spit polish.

"Oh, Holly." She clasped her hands together. "I've been looking for your ex-husband all day."

I wanted to correct her. I liked to call him my ex-ass, but held my tongue. I wanted to get all the information I could, so when I did find him, I could kill him myself.

"I was hoping you could help me." I said, and jumped out of the way, as Agnes swung open the screen door.

Agnes motioned for me to come in and led me down the light blue hallway into what looked like a kitchen and family room combination. Only, there was still a partial wall between the two rooms with exposed wires sticking out.

I'm no expert, but I think that was just a tad bit unsafe.

Agnes moved around exactly the way I remembered. She crept around the kitchen cleaning up what looked like the remnants of breakfast. The sound of the percolating coffee sounded inviting, but the smell was even better.

"Help you with what, honey?" Agnes asked.

"I'm looking for that no good ex-husband of mine, and I thought he said he was coming here this morning." I lied.

Sean didn't tell me he was working here, but Agnes didn't know that.

"I need to get my alimony money to pay my rent." I continued to lie. "But he's not here?"

It would seem like I was up to something if I told her the truth.

"Haven't seen him. I even had Marlene drive over to his house, but she said he didn't answer the door and his truck wasn't there." Agnes poured herself a cup of coffee without offering me a cup.

"What time did he say he was coming?" I wanted to know exactly what he said.

I replayed what Agnes had said at the Diva meeting about Sean killing Doug for more business. It just didn't add up. Sean would never kill just to pay me alimony. He would do anything not to go to jail, and I had threatened to turn him in on several occasions. I wasn't really going to do it, and harmless threats are just that. . .harmless.

Until someone shows up dead on your floor.

"He came over and looked at what that no good Doug Sloan did and gave me an estimate to fix it." Agnes pointed to the half wall and broken kitchen tiles. "Said he would be here early this morning. I got up and got ready."

Agnes ran her hand over her turban and flicked the feather.

"That's the last you heard from him?" I asked, trying to jog her memory.

"Not a peep since. Sean's always been here on time when he says he's coming." She tapped her wristwatch. The numbers were so big that I could see it from where I was standing. "That's why I sent Marlene over with a batch of my fudge."

Ah, that was what she was cleaning up. I saw her delicious chocolate fudge on the cooling rack on the counter. My mouth watered, because I knew Marlene would be bringing some to munch on at the shop, and I'd get a piece.

"Where is Marlene?" I looked around and listened closely.

She couldn't be far. The yellow gem she toted around was propped up all nice and shiny on the marble mantel, as though it were on display.

Sean had something to say about Marlene before the tape was shredded, and I needed to find out what it was.

If she were around, I would have heard her heels clicking on Agnes' hardwood floors.

Agnes walked into the family room and almost sat on the glass coffee table, until I gently guided her to the chair.

"Oh, thank you. My eyes aren't as good as they use to be." She pushed the turban a bit to the left. "Have you lost weight, Holly Harper?"

I straightened my shoulders and sat up a little taller. Did she really notice some weight loss? Had all my work started to pay off?

"I've been working really hard to." I confirmed. "I've been walking Willow around the lake, and meeting Bernadine to walk when she can."

Agnes reached over and took her glasses off the side table. I jumped when she looked at me. They magnified her eyes ten times.

"There." She opened and closed her eyes as if she was trying to bring the room into focus. Her eyes narrowed. "No, I guess you haven't. I tell you, my eyesight is about shot."

If I could've become one with the couch, I would have. I slumped down into the cushions.

"Go on. Take a look at what that Doug Sloan did to my house." Agnes adjusted her turban again. "I think it's awful, them saying you killed Doug Sloan and framing Sean for it."

"They said? Who said?" I asked, trying to steady my heart to keep it from leaping out of my chest.

There wasn't strong enough evidence to charge me. Well, they did find the body that was strangled with my beads in my shop. I guess I'd believe I did too, if I weren't me.

"All you have to do is give them your cell phone." Agnes rocked back in forth in the rocking recliner.

"Why would a cell phone help?" Now I knew Agnes Pearl wasn't only blind, but out of her mind.

She mumbled a few words, but my mind and eyes couldn't stop looking at that yellow Spinel propped up on the mantel for everyone and their brother to see. Marlene had been carrying it around with her since the day I first laid eyes on her, and never let it out of her sight.

Odd.

There had to be some story behind it, otherwise, she wouldn't want to disguise it in a beading wrap.

"What did you say about a cell phone?" I asked again, taking my eyes off the sparkler to concentrate on what Agnes had to say.

"I said they can track your cell phone. Don't you keep it on you?" She looked at me like I had two heads.

Embarrassed, I tilted my head down in shame.

"Um, I don't have a cell phone." I mumbled.

"Who doesn't have a cell phone these days?" Agnes scolded me. "Damn. I guess you are a suspect if they can't place you anywhere else."

This cell phone situation was really becoming an issue. Maybe I need to take a trip over to Cell City Shop and at least take a look at them.

Agnes eased herself out of the recliner and moseyed into the kitchen. She refilled her mug and then stared out the window. She did seem a bit nervous; I could see she was rubbing her hands together.

"Where is Marlene?" I asked, and walked up behind Agnes.

I had to know what Sean wanted to tell me. Maybe Marlene was a piece of the puzzle.

Peering over her shoulder, and looking into the luscious garden, I saw Marlene with a shovel and a man wearing a gardening hat.

"There she is." I stepped back and headed toward the back door.

"Marlene!" I waved to her from the back door.

She said a couple of words to the man, peeled off her hot pink gardening gloves, and walked up to the house.

"Holly, what a nice surprise." Marlene's jaw clenched with every chew on the wad of gum in her mouth.

"We need to talk." I walked out the door and turned to face her. "Did you talk to Sean?"

"Yes. He was here yesterday to give Agnes an estimate on the kitchen." She wrapped the gum around her pointer finger, and stuck it back in her mouth.

"Pearl said you went over to his house and he wasn't there." I wanted to confirm that I had Agnes' story straight.

As sane as she might seem, some days, Agnes did get details mixed up.

"When he didn't show up, Agnes wanted me to check on him," she said, and then blew a bubble.

"Did you and Sean talk?" The message he left on my machine was starting to haunt me. "He left me a message and said your name right before the machine ate the tape."

"He wanted to know if I had anyone who could get him an out-of-town job." She said.

"And…" I arched my eyebrows, indicating that I needed more information.

"I told him about a couple places in towns where I used to live that might be interested." She shrugged her shoulders.

None of what she was saying made any sense. If he needed work, he could stay in Swanee because he was the only contractor available with Doug…well, six feet under. If he needed to leave town, that was another issue entirely.

"Where exactly would that be?" I asked.

As I thought about it, I couldn't recall her ever telling me or any of the other Divas where she was from.

"Over in South Burrow." She gestured like the two hour car ride was right across town. "When he didn't show up today, I figured he went there. Noah even stopped by to talk to him, and of course, Agnes said he was missing. She spilled her guts."

Marlene leaned in a little closer.

"Between you and me, I bet that good for nothing ex of yours killed Doug and the heat is on. I think he skipped town." Marlene whispered and nodded her head.

"Marlene, that's not Sean's style." I whispered back.

"Desperate times bring out the worst in people." She batted those fake lashes, and cracked her gum. "You said he's been acting strange."

I took a step back, and looked closely at Marlene. How do I know she wasn't trying to take the heat off herself? And I had yet to ask about her meeting with the two women at the pier.

"Hey, do you think you could go open the shop? I'll pay you overtime." I said, hoping to entice her.

I knew I couldn't afford to pay Marlene overtime, but I had no time to waste. I had to find Sean.

"When you do talk to Sean, tell him he needs to come get this work done. Agnes already paid him for it." Marlene blew one last bubble before she walked into the house and let the door slam behind her.

"Hi." I waved to the gardener on my way out.

Before getting into my car, Jim and Ginger's van pulled up and parked in Agnes' driveway. I waited by my car for her to get out.

"What are you doing here?" I looked back and forth between the two of them.

"Agnes wants a couple security cameras installed. We're getting calls left and right." Ginger put her hand on my arm. "Holly, you should really think about getting cameras for the shop."

"I'll think about it." I knew it would be a good idea, but they cost so much.

"We're going to put cameras in the barn and possibly on the outside of the cabin." Jim said.

Ginger hit him on the arm.

"What?" Jim's forehead curled as he spoke to Ginger. "I told you to tell her."

"It's no big deal." I couldn't believe Ginger hadn't told me. "It's your property. I've got to get going."

I waved and put on a fake smile before getting into my car. I was a little annoyed at the fact they were putting in security cameras at the cottage. I understood they were looking out for their property, but what about my privacy? Doesn't that count for something?

Noah Druck needs to solve this case fast before the whole town turns on each other, wondering if their neighbors killed Doug. One person was holding the answers I needed.

Sean.

What would Veronica Mars do? Would she go to South Burrow to find Sean or wait for him to show up?

The last time I went to South Burrow was right before The Beaded Dragonfly opened. The South Burrow Daily interviewed me about being the only lapidary in the area. In order to see the article, I had to go to South Burrow and buy the paper at the Piggly Wiggly.

Yep.

It looked like I was making a trip to South Burrow before self-defense class tonight.

Chapter Twenty-two

I tried calling Sean a few more times before I finally made my decision to drive the two hours to South Burrow. I still hadn't gotten a hold of him, and I was beginning to panic.

In a moment of weakness, I called Ginger's and left a message for Jim to meet me at the shop later this afternoon. It was time to invest in those cameras.

I didn't dare tell her I was going to South Burrow to hunt for Sean. She'd only try to talk me out of it and tell me that Marlene was trying to take the heat off herself.

Even if Marlene was involved, Sean's behavior was out of character.

The two-hour drive didn't help to clear my head. I came up with all sorts of scenarios on why someone would kill Doug and who would want to. It still didn't make sense for Sean to do it, but if he'd really left town, he had to know something.

South Burrow had always been known for having a cozy atmosphere and close neighbors. It was half the size of Swanee. If Sean was in town, someone would have seen him.

I made my way through South Burrow taking in all the mom and pop shops to check if Sean had stopped into any of them. I made a mental note on a few more to hit on my way back out of town.

I pulled into what looked like was the last used car lot at the very edge of town. It seemed like a good place to turn around and begin my search. Out of the corner of my eye I saw a red and white old Chevy truck that looked a lot Sean's.

I put my car in reverse and backed up to the truck. I got out and slowly walked around it, taking in every nook and cranny. On the door, I ran my finger along the outline of where a magnetic sign used to be.

"Runs good." The voice behind me called out. "You need a good work truck? I've got all the paper work including oil changes."

My heart pounded. Sean took immaculate care of his beloved Chevy, all the way down to changing the oil every three thousand miles. This was definitely Sean's truck.

"It's been well taken care of." I smiled and patted the hood. "Why in the world would someone want to get rid of a good looking truck like this?"

"He said that he was moving to the city and he wouldn't need a truck anymore. Even walked back into town." The salesman pointed toward South Burrow and then leaned up against the door. "You new to South Burrow?"

"I was just passing through and I hadn't seen a truck like this in such good condition." I dragged my hand along the lines of the truck and stopped at the door. "Looks like something was here, like a magnet or something."

"Yeah, he took that." The salesman took a hanky out of his pocket and began to spit shine the outline. "Something about handyman or something with a house on it."

I felt faint. Sean had really done it. He killed Doug Sloan and left me to take the blame.

I walked in a daze back to my car.

"Miss? You want to test drive it?" The salesman called out.

I started my car and peeled out of the lot. Something wasn't right. No matter how logical it all seemed, for the two-hour ride back to Swanee, I couldn't rationalize how Sean could've done this.

I had to check his house. He had to have left something behind.

I pulled up to Sean's and looked around before I got out of the car. Everything looked the same about the brick ranch. The dried flower stems were still sticking up out of the dirt in the flower boxes underneath each window. The bushes were overgrown, and the lawn was as tall as a small child.

Yep, still looked the same. Nothing out of the ordinary.

Walking past the windows, I checked each one to see if any of them happened to be unlocked. It didn't seem natural to be breaking into the house I once lived in.

Then it dawned on me. I picked up the gnome next to the third bush on the left. There it was, just as shiny as ever. The extra key that I put there years ago without Sean even knowing.

Wow, how life seems to come full circle. I picked up the key, remembering I had it made at Sloan's Hardware, and Doug was the one who was working that day.

I held the key tight and squeezed my eyes closed. I prayed Sean hadn't changed the locks.

I slipped the key in and like magic, the lock turned.

I flicked on the light, and found the usual bachelor pad squalor Sean had turned the joint into. Empty pizza boxes, knocked over Bud Lights, and the chandelier still in the box.

"I knew it!" I screamed running over to the box.

Carefully I looked in and the chandelier was still there, right where Sean keeps it. There was definitely something fishy. There was no way Sean would leave town without this precious heirloom. Or as he said, "Over my dead body."

I shivered.

"Sean, please don't be dead." I whispered into the air, and began to look around the family room and then into the kitchen for any clues to where he might be.

I searched for a note, anything with a scribble, a business card, anything. I even looked at his phone to see who the last person was he called. . .me. There was a pink piece of paper that looked to be a carbon copy from a doctor's office.

I folded it and tucked it and the key in my pants pocket. I wasn't comfortable being here, and if he was missing, they could be watching me.

I grabbed the chandelier box, because I didn't want anyone to steal it from him, and backed my way out of the house. With the door shut tight, I twisted the knob to make sure it was locked, and then turned to get in my car.

"What do we have here?" Noah stood in the grass with his hand rested on his holster.

"Hey, Noah." I nonchalantly continued to my car.

"Is Sean home?" Noah craned his neck to get a peek inside the box. I held it closer to me "What's in the box?"

"Just my chandelier that Sean was keeping for me until I was ready to put it up in the shop," I lied.

Noah looked past me at the house.

"So, Sean's home?" He walked around me toward the door.

"Well, no. Good seeing you." I quickly walked ahead, only to be stopped.

"Wait. Sean's not here. You are. You have a key?" Noah face changed as if he was thinking.

"I did live here, Noah." I hoped he'd fall for it, but I was wrong.

"You and I both know Sean doesn't want you in that house when he's not here. So what are you hiding, Holly?" Noah crossed his arms. "Sean? Are you hiding Sean?"

"Don't be ridiculous, Noah." I laughed out loud hoping to throw him off track, but it came out as nervous laughter. "Hiding Sean? You know I would've done that a long time ago if I could."

I tucked the box under my arm while getting my keys ready to unlock my car.

"And you think you are just going to get in your car without answering some questions first?" Noah asked.

I opened the passenger door and carefully sat the box in the seat. If there was ever going to be a time that I would be able to get that chandelier, this was it, and no one was going to stop me.

I shut the door and walked back toward Noah, who was writing in that damn notebook again.

"Listen, I don't know what you write in that little pad of paper you got there, but I do know that I don't know where Sean is. I'm not his keeper." I put my hands on my hips. "I'm leaving. You don't have any type of warrant to keep me here. I also didn't kill Doug or Sean, for that matter."

I stomped back to the car. Before I could get in, Noah cleared his throat. I looked back at him.

"Holly, I never said anything about killing Doug or Sean." A smile crept across his face like he knew something I didn't. "You can be sure I'll be stopping by to see you real soon."

He nodded, tilting his hat towards me as if he was being a gentleman.

I rolled my eyes at his not-so-subtle threat and got into my car. I had to get back to the shop before anyone else began to suspect that I was up to something.

Chapter Twenty-three

Marlene was putting away the new shipment that had come in overnight. After finding Sean's truck and things just not adding up, I had to ask Marlene about the women, the notes, and the pier.

"Marlene, last week I was…" I couldn't tell the whole truth, "walking around the lake and saw you talking to a couple women by the pier."

Her mouth opened, and then she closed it shut. Tight.

"I yelled your name, but you didn't hear me." I picked up the pencil and pretended to jot down a few notes on the cash receipts by the register.

"I was meeting someone. I forgot about you living way out there." She was checking off items on the inventory sheet. "Shh, I can't count with all this talking."

Nothing made sense. Sean seemed to have skipped town, leaving me to take the blame. Marlene leaves me a couple of crazy notes and then doesn't act any different toward me or the Divas.

The silence was broken by the ringing of the bell above the shop door.

"Hi, Jim." Marlene chomped away. "You in here to get something for Ginger?"

Jim was shy. He never said much around the Divas. Probably in fear we'd knock him down with the ex's.

"I came to talk to Holly about some video cameras." He held up some equipment.

I'd completely forgotten that I had told Ginger to send Jim over. There was a time when no one in Swanee needed video cameras to keep an eye on their belongings or a keep one eye open at night out of fear they were going to get murdered.

"Holly, I asked Sean to stop by the lumber yard for a few new material quotes, and he never showed." Jim sat the cameras on the counter. "Do you know how I can get in touch with him? It sounded pretty urgent when he called."

The last thing Sean would do would take charity from the Sloan's. And if he really did skip town, he wouldn't have put an order in for new materials.

"Nope, haven't seen or heard from him," I said, making a mental note on why Sean would need charity. "And I probably won't. Alimony time."

Alimony was becoming a good excuse for everyone.

Marlene cackled. "Maybe he won't be back."

I shot her a look. Why would she say that? Did she really know he was gone somewhere?

Jim rolled his eyes. I'm sure Ginger has told him all about Marlene. I smiled and blew her off. After all, it was Marlene.

"We can go in the back." I didn't want to disturb all the customers who were sitting down to quietly bead. "Follow me."

Week, week, week, Willow squealed when I pushed her off the loveseat. She loved lying in the patch of the sunshine. She snorted a few times and sat by Jim's feet. She nudged him like he was supposed to be petting her.

He complied.

"I sure do hate what happened to Doug." I felt like I needed to apologize for finding him in my shop. "I mean, I didn't do it."

Jim shook his head and bit his bottom lip.

I'd never seen a grown man cry, and I didn't want to then.

"We know it wasn't you. That'd be a little too obvious. And I know a lot of people didn't like Doug, but deep down, he was really a good kid." He held back tears. "He didn't deserve to die. No one does."

I agreed, in spite of all the problems he'd caused for Ginger and Jim. No matter how many times Doug messed up, Jim always came to his rescue. Jim even sent "hush" work Sean's way.

Of course, Sean never told me, but Ginger did. She would secretly complain about Doug.

Jim showed me several camera options, but I needed something on the cheaper end of the spectrum. Two cameras placed strategically in the shop would be sufficient. I decided on the cheapest service option also. Jim's company would host the feed; therefore, I wouldn't have any of the recording equipment in the shop. If something funny happened or the shop got broken into again, the police could get the footage from Jim's company directly.

I signed up for a three-month trial. Hopefully, by the end of that time, I could cancel because Sean would be back, and Doug's killer would be behind bars.

"Bye, Jim." Marlene leaned over the counter.

Jim blushed. Marlene's low-cut top showed more than anyone wanted to see, but Marlene didn't care.

"He told Agnes that everyone has been calling him. Seems like the whole town is afraid they're going to be next." Marlene dragged her long fingernail across her throat as if she was slitting it.

"I have to go to self-defense class." I looked her square in the eyes. "I'm not done talking with you about that night at the pier. I'm giving you the benefit of the doubt, but some people in town think you are suspicious."

It was time I gave it Marlene straight. There were questions that needed to be answered and I was tired of tiptoeing around her.

"There is a logical explanation for everything. I promise." There was a terrified look on her face. "I didn't have anything to do with Doug's death, or Sean going missing. I don't know anything about that."

"For some strange reason, I believe you. But I don't understand these." I pulled the notes out of the counter drawer where I had been hiding them.

She read them carefully, taking big gulps the whole time.

"Please just give me one more day. I promise I will tell you everything." She put her hands together as if she was begging.

"Fine." I held my finger up in the air before leaving for my self-defense class. "One more day."

I trotted down the steps and jumped into the car to head to the Moose.

It was a pleasant surprise to see Cheri, Flora, and Bernadine in the front of the class. I went to the bathroom and quickly changed into my yoga pants.

Ouch. Something had poked me. I checked the small pocket on the inside of my pants where I had forgotten I put Sean's extra house key and the pink paper that reminded me of the doctor's office. I didn't wash my pants every time I wear them. This kept them stretched out, making me feel like I'd lost more inches than I really had.

"What are y'all doing here?" I pulled my arms over my head like I was an old pro at stretching out.

"Living alone with a killer on the loose? It's a no brainer for me." Flora said.

She did live alone in an upscale condominium complex on the east side of town, but she was surrounded by plenty of men who could help protect her.

"Hey, where is your phone?" I put my hand on my heart as if I was going to have a heart attack.

"Funny, Holly." Flora rolled her eyes and did a few squats.

"Where have you been?" I asked Bernadine. "Willow and I have missed you on our walks."

"I had to run a few errands. And I didn't want to bother your little visit with Marlene." She tried to do a few toe touches, but could only make it to her knees.

"Marlene?" I questioned her.

"I saw Marlene over at your place yesterday." Bernadine took a couple deep breathes before plunging back down towards her toes.

No matter how much Bernadine huffed and puffed, she could only reach her knees.

What on earth was she talking about? Marlene hadn't been to my house in weeks, that I could remember, unless you want to count the night at the pier.

Marlene was working for mc yesterday. I had to think back to what the schedule was. It seemed that Marlene was working a lot for me at that time. I'd rather have her at work so I could keep an eye her, because something wasn't right with her, just like something wasn't right with Sean.

"Oh, yeah." I lied to the Divas, and stretched my arms behind me. "Come to think of it, she did stop by for a few minutes."

Cheri sat on the floor with her legs in a "v" formation and stretched to each side. We all stopped and stared at her in amazement. I don't think any of us could touch our knees with our noses.

"What did she want?" Cheri asked, looking up and resting her ear on her knee. "Did she mention anything about the other night at the pier?"

Ah, to be young and thin. . .

"Um, she wanted to know when she worked next." I did a few squats, and pretended to keep my eyes on my shoes.

I didn't want to look at any of them for fear my face would give me away. I was getting pretty good at lying. I crossed my fingers behind my back.

"That's weird that your shop wasn't open." Flora rolled her body around in circles while keeping her feet planted on the floor. "Besides, doesn't she just work when you call her?"

"Noah had to look at something, so the shop was closed for a bit." Technically that wasn't a lie. Noah did close the shop for a little bit, just a few days earlier.

I had to get out of this line of questioning before they caught me in a lie. I could tell they were already suspicious by their questions.

"I've got to pee." I jogged off, acting like I was really into the class, but truth be told, I'd rather have been on my futon watching Veronica Mars.

Hopefully, by the time I got back, Mancho Man would have started the class, and the Divas would be too busy learning defense moves to even think about Marlene.

"Whoa!" A voice boomed, and two strong hands gripped the sides of my arms to stop me from colliding with the person they were attached to.

Only it was too late. My face had already planted into Mancho Man's pecs.

"I, um, I'm sorry." I could feel my face flush.

"What was the first think I taught you last week?" His six foot four inch frame towered over me. He was standing with his arms crossed.

"Keys!" I snapped my fingers Ha! I did listen.

"No, Holly, not keys." There was disappointment in his brown eyes. "Be aware of your surroundings at all times."

I smacked my forehead. Hell, if I couldn't do that, how was I going to do something as simple as find Sean or something as difficult as exonerating both of us of Doug's murder?

"Sorry, I need to pee." I lied. . .again.

"Hurry up. I'm about to start class, and I don't want you to miss the robber hold." He pointed me in the direction of the bathroom. "Holly?"

I crossed my legs like I had to pee, and did a little bouncing up and down.

"Yes?" I realized I didn't know his name.

"I'd be happy to give you private classes since you are having all this trouble lately." He smiled, which he should do more off. "Cheri told me about all the break-ins."

"I'll think about it." There was no way I was going to let anyone else in on everything that was going on. The less he knew, the better. "Hey, what is your name?"

"Donovan. Donovan Scott." He smiled again, before he disappeared into the group of students waiting for him.

I couldn't look at any of the Divas during class out of fear that I'd burst out laughing. We had to be the most uncoordinated bunch of middle-aged broads I'd ever seen.

On several occasions, Donovan had to tell Flora to silence her cell phone. Finally, after it had gone off several more times, he came over and took it from her. I thought she was going to have a heart attack when he shut it off and held it over his head when she tried to jump up to get it. She didn't give up without a fight, but in the end, she lost the battle.

"I can see how this could help me tone my arms like yours." Flora flexed, referring to Cheri.

"It would help if we were a little younger." Bernadine flicked the flab under her arm as she flexed.

I was sure my arms were going to be sore tomorrow. Donovan had us in positions that no robber would ever put me in.

He asked us to split off into pairs. Bernadine grabbed me, which was a huge mistake.

"What did Marlene *really* want?" She whispered as she put in me in the robber hold.

For this particular defense move, I was supposed to play the victim and head butt the robber, Bernadine, held me from behind, gripping my wrist with one of her hands and holding me close with her other arm wrapped around me.

She was also supposed to say, "Give me your money," but decided it was time to get the truth out of me.

"I can tell you are lying, Holly Harper." Bernadine was making up her own dialog using her best robber voice.

"I told you." I winced from her ring that was cutting into my wrist. I jerked. "Let go."

"Good, good." Donovan nodded and smiled walking by all the pairs.

"I'm not letting go until you tell me the truth." Bernadine squeezed harder.

She was getting really good at this robber act.

"Let go now!" I yelled and stomped my foot down. I could've head butted her like I were supposed to, but I didn't want to hurt her.

"Ewwwowl!" Bernadine screamed. She let go of me, grabbed her toe and hopped around on one foot. "You smashed my toe."

I tried to rub the ring indentions off my wrist but they were too deep. Donovan jogged over to see what all the commotion was about.

"She. . ." Bernadine had her shoe off and was rubbing her perfectly-pedicure red toenails. "Holly decided to stomp on my foot, for real!"

"You were holding me a little too tight." I held my wrist out to show Donovan.

"Now ladies, we're only pretending here." He looked back and forth between us. Before he walked off, he said, "Good job, though."

"Geesh." Bernadine continued to rub her big toe. "Now I know you were lying and I'm going to find out what it's about."

"Come over later and we can talk." I took a look at her toe. There was some red nail polish that had been chipped off. "I'm sorry."

We both started to laugh. Everyone turned to look at us, which made us laugh even harder.

Before I changed back into my pants, Donovan asked again if I wanted one on one lessons. I told him again that I'd think about it, but we exchanged numbers anyway. It wouldn't hurt to have extra protection, and I'd have his number just in case.

Chapter Twenty-four

Sean had been on my mind all day. It wouldn't do me any good to stop by his house now that I knew his truck had been sold in South Burrow.

On the way home, I decided to take a detour and stop at Sloan's Hardware to take advantage of the pay phone.

Ten, fifteen, twenty...damn. There wasn't enough change in my ashtray to pay for a call, but I was sure there had to be some loose change somewhere in the car. I didn't bother checking my wallet, because I knew it was dry as a bone, so I checked under the floor mats, in the console, and glove box and came up with nothing.

Out of the corner of my eye, I saw a flash of silver between the driver's seat and console. There it was, barely sticking out.

I surveyed how it was positioned. I was sure if I went under my seat, I could get it. *Under..ugh!*

I opted to grab the pen I'd seen in the glove box and started flicking at what little of the coin was visible.

I flung my body against the seat, and held the pen out like a weapon when someone knocked on my window.

Be aware of your surroundings. I had to post that somewhere.

"You alright?" Jim motioned for me to roll down the window.

"Jim, you scared the crap out of me." I said as I rolled it down. "Between you and Ginger, I might be the next person in the morgue due to a heart attack."

"I saw you over here, so I thought I'd walk over to see how the cameras are doing," He said, and waved to someone driving past. "What are you doing in there?"

"I was going to call Sean, but I didn't have enough change. I was looking for some." I threw my hands up in the air.

Jim dug in the front of his blue, blue jeans, and pulled out some coins.

"You know, Ginger makes me keep this phone booth here for you. It costs me more to keep it than you use it." Jim handed me the money. "You really should get a cell phone. Not that I'm trying to act like your husband looking after you, but I am your best friend's husband and she thinks you should have one too."

"Yeah, yeah." I put the coins in the slot and carefully dialed Sean's mobile.

I had to concentrate on pushing the right numbers because I couldn't risk dialing the wrong number like I had done so many times before. This time, I couldn't afford to screw up, literally.

"Sean, it's Hol." I thought if I called myself by the nickname he had given me when we were married, he might feel some emotion and return my call. Wishful thinking, but it was worth a try. "I saw your truck in South Burrow. Please call me. We can work this out."

Not that I really wanted to fix our relationship, but I did want to find him to take the heat off of me.

"So, you still haven't seen him?" Jim asked. "Why is his truck in South Burrow?"

I hadn't realized he was still standing there.

Really, everything seemed to be running together. Days, nights, and hours.

"Tell me about South Burrow." Jim seemed awfully curious.

I'm sure he was trying to gather any information he could to help with the investigation, including taking in everything I was saying. I'd made it a point not to tell Ginger anything.

"I had to go there for some beads and I saw his truck there." I lied yet again. "Marlene had told him about some work down there."

"South Burrow? What does Marlene know about South Burrow?" He asked, and then waved at another hardware customer.

"Apparently she's from there." I got back in my car. "I guess I better go."

Jim walked back to the shop, and I headed for home.

I racked my brain for any clue why Sean would leave town. When I talked to him before he disappeared, I had been sure he was innocent. Since he sold his precious truck, it's made me question whether I really knew him at all. The only evidence that he hadn't left for good was his precious chandelier he'd left behind. That was enough of a red flag for me to question where he really was.

I glanced at the box in the back seat in my rearview mirror. There was no way Sean would leave town without that box, guilty or not.

There was foul play somewhere in all of this.

I tapped my fingers on the steering wheel and tried to piece all the information I had. Unfortunately, the pieces of the puzzle were not fitting together. Plus it was hard to concentrate with all the honking horns behind me.

The new ePhone was coming out today, and it looked like everyone in Swanee was turning into Cell City's parking lot.

With all the excitement, I found myself turning in with them.

I convinced myself it wouldn't hurt to look and followed the people into the shop.

A lady in a blue Cell City t-shirt greeted me as soon as I walked in the sliding glass doors.

"Welcome to Cell City." She smiled, and handed me a brochure with a picture of the new ePhone on the front. "Are you here to get the new ePhone?"

I shrugged. "I'm just checking it out."

Before I knew what was happening, she had me sitting in a cubicle, signing a two-year contract, and explaining how I could tell this phone what to do by just talking to it.

"Like solve a murder?" I asked, hoping the new gadget could return my life back to normal.

"No." She threw her head back in laughter. "Oh, you are a funny one."

Within minutes, I was out the door, sitting in my car with my new ePhone.

Immediately, I dialed Sean's number, knowing he never answers a call from a number he doesn't recognize. But I thought if I gave him the option to call my new phone, he might call me back.

I'd never considered that Noah might be tapping my home or shop phone until that moment. I wouldn't put it past him.

This is Sean. I'm going to be out of town putting up chandeliers in a new restaurant. So leave a message and I'll eventually get back to you.

What? I hung up and redialed. He put a new message on his phone between the time I'd called from Sloan's Hardware phone booth and this time?

I listened carefully.

He sounded tired, withdrawn.

I called back. I needed to write down every single word in his message. I grabbed a pen from the glove box, and with no time to find a piece of paper, I wrote on my arm.

Out of town, chandelier, eventually.

Those words spoken in his tired voice replayed in my head when I hung up. Those words were completely out of character for him.

One, he almost never left Swanee. Not even on our honeymoon. As a matter of fact, we never took a honeymoon.

Two, he said chandelier. What man says chandelier? Also, why go into so much detail in an outgoing message? Was that a clue? Was he in trouble and he knew I'd be calling to talk to him?

Deep down, I had to believe he put those words on there for me to hear. He was in trouble, and I had to find him.

And three, eventually was always *right now* for him. Sean loved to work. He jumped at the chance to work every time. So, if someone did call him for an job, he would always call them back right away, no matter what, and give them a time frame when he could get the job done.

Out of town, chandelier, eventually. I continued to repeat those words out loud until I got home.

Chapter Twenty-five

"Hello?" Bernadine answered her phone; there was a little trepidation in her voice.

"Bernadine, I'm so glad you are home. Do you want to go for a walk?" I asked.

I wanted to talk out what was going on in my head. I've already conjured up every scenario, from Sean being a murderer and running off, to him being kidnapped.

Bernadine had always been the most logical Diva other than Ginger. And talking to Ginger wasn't an option at this point.

"I don't know. I'm awfully tired, and my toe still hurts." Bernadine said. "Where are you calling from?"

"I got the new ePhone." I never thought those words would come out of my mouth. And by Bernadine's silence, she obviously didn't either.

"You what?" Bernadine finally broke the silence.

I imagined her jumping up and down with excitement.

"Yes, I broke down and got one." I briefly told her about my adventure in Cell City. "Listen, I really need to talk to you."

Before I made it home, Bernadine had already used my hidden key and let herself in. She and Willow were sitting on the futon. Willow had her snoot stuck deep down into Bernadine's zip lock baggie of treats and eating her heart out.

Bernadine claimed that Food Watchers told her if she carried around healthy snacks, it would aid in her weight loss plan. I think the snacks were meant for Bernadine to eat, not Willow.

"Bernadine, I told you that she can't eat all those grapes." I took the bag and put it on the counter.

The last time Willow ate Bernadine's grapes, she had diarrhea for a week. Doc Johnson, Swanee's only veterinarian, had a hard time getting Willow regulated.

"Well, let's see it." Bernadine held out her hand. "I want to hold the new ePhone. I hear it can do anything short of cooking."

I laughed, and handed her the new electronic gadget. For the price of the darn thing, it should be doing my laundry.

Bernadine played with my new phone while I went to my bedroom to change into my walking stretch pants.

I slipped them on and looked in the mirror. They felt looser, and they were. I even had to double over the waistband. I slipped my tennies on and skipped down the hall.

"You ready?" I looked down at Willow.

He-hon, he-hon, he-hon, She trotted over to the hook where her beaded collar and hot pink leash hung, her tail twirling with excitement. She had already figured out that when I put those stretch pants on and followed up with my tennis shoes, she was going for a walk.

It took us two times around the lake for me to tell Bernadine everything I knew about Sean and Marlene.

"I can't believe that." Bernadine seemed amazed at all that had taken place. "How much is the Spinel diamond?"

I stopped dead in my tracks, and turned to face her.

"Are you kidding me?" I asked her, a tad bit frustrated. "I just told you that I believed something has happened to Sean and all you can think about is how much Marlene's gem is worth?"

"It's a lot to take in. Besides, isn't this what we Divas do? Wish our exes away?" Bernadine smiled and shoved me when I didn't reciprocate. "Come on, Holly, we will find him."

"Well, don't tell any of the Divas anything I told you." I stumbled from Willow pulling so hard to get back to the cottage. "Are you sure you saw Marlene here?"

"I'm double-dog positive. On my ex-husbands pension." Bernadine made the sign of the cross, because God knows there was no way Bernadine would pit anything against the big payout she was going to be getting.

Willow went straight to the water dish. She wasn't use to so much exercise.

A knock at the door made us jump. The clock read 9pm, which was late for me to get a visitor. Unless it was Sean.

"Sean?" I swung the front door open with hope in my heart.

"Wrong." Noah Druck stood on the small concrete slab just outside the door.

What does he want? I mouthed to Bernadine. She didn't wait to answer me. She grabbed her things and hurried out the door.

"Hi, Noah." She gave a spirited wave. "Bye, Noah."

What a good Diva she was. Leaving me high and dry. She made the phone symbol with her hand and held it up to her ear, "*Call me,*" she mouthed back.

We watched Bernadine hurry to her rowboat so she could row back to her side of the lake.

"Come on in." I held the door wide open.

Willow snorted as though she was asking him to come in. He looked at her and then at me.

"I'll stay out here. This is official police business." He rested his hands on his hips. "Tell me about Sean's truck in South Burrow."

My mouth dropped, and then I quickly shut it. That no-good-for-nothing Jim Rush must've ran straight to the police station after I spilled the beans about the truck.

Dirty rat.

"If you don't tell me, it doesn't matter." He leaned in like he was going to let me in on a little secret. "I will be making a trip to South Burrow tomorrow."

Maybe Noah finding out about the truck was a good thing. I could tell him about the truck, voicemail, chandelier, everything, and maybe he could put out an APB and find Sean.

Just as I was about the spill the beans, a cell phone rang.

Girls, girls, girls, Vince Neal and Motely Crew belted out the ring tone loud and clear.

Yes, it was so eighties, but it was Sean's favorite song and long-time ring tone.

My eyes grew when the phone continued to sing in my cottage. Willow ran back to the bedroom. Was Sean here? Had he been here?

"Holly, you and I both know that is Sean's ring tone." He walked past me and into the cottage. "Where is he?"

The phone rang again. *Girls, girls, girls.*

"I have no idea where he is or where the phone is." I made one last attempt to draw his attention away from the ringing phone.

By the look on Noah's face, he wasn't buying it. So I went in search of Vince's voice. As I got closer, it stopped.

"Holly, I'm not playing games." He was on my heels. "If Sean killed Doug, you are an accessory to murder. Unless *you* killed Doug, and Sean found out. Then you'd have to put some of those Diva ideas into motion. If that was the case, I'm sure you know where Sean is."

Noah plucked his cell from its case that was attached to his uniform belt, and typed on the keypad.

Girls, girls, girls.

I stood still as if cement was in my shoes. Someone was setting me up, that was for sure. I watched Noah walk over to the futon and run his hand along the creases. I cringed, thinking about his hands in *The Under*, but he didn't mind.

"Look what I found." Noah held the phone up and tucked it in his jacket pocket. "And to think, all these years you never put your hand *under* anything."

"That's right!" I pointed to the futon. "I didn't know it was there. I would never put anything in an *under*."

"I'm going to give you forty-eight hours to get your story straight and talk to a lawyer. And you need to include the little incident from this afternoon at Sean's house." His eyes squinted as if he was trying to read me.

I knew not to say a word. There was nothing I could say to get me out of this mess.

Noah walked back to his cruiser without looking back.

I shut the door, locked it, and checked it twice. Chills went all over my body. I pulled back the curtains and glanced outside. I wondered who was watching me. Who knew to call Sean's phone when Noah was here? Someone wanted Noah to find it here. Who was that someone?

That someone had been in my cottage and planted Sean's cell phone in my futon.

Ouch. I felt in the small pocket of my yoga pants to see what poked me, and it was Sean's key and piece of paper that I had stolen from his house. I took out the pink carbon copy paper and unfolded it.

Allergy tests results? I read the paper aloud. Sean was allergy tested? I recalled him sneezing in The Beaded Dragonfly after the Divas' and I had gone to Ginger's to give our condolences.

Damn, if he weren't missing, I would secretly wish he was allergic to me. But it only stated he was allergic to the typical things: mold, pollen, cocoa...*cocoa*!

Now I knew I was right. Sean was in trouble. Someone was setting me up for the murder of Doug Sloan, and that someone kidnapped Sean.

Chapter Twenty-six

Thank goodness I'd asked Marlene to open the shop, because when Willow nudged me, the clock read 10am.

She nudged me again. I pushed her snout away from my armpit.

"Okay, let's go." I said, and got out off the futon.

The TV was tuned to the local morning news.

Last night after I got home, I was scared to death. So much so that I couldn't sleep and decided to practice some of the new self-defense moves I had learned. I even put in a Veronica Mars DVD.

Somehow, Veronica always made me feel better, or at least she gave me a few ideas on where to start looking for Sean.

I felt like I'd given Marlene enough time to come clean, and I wanted to know who those women from the pier were. I also wanted to know why she had stopped by the cottage when she was supposed to be working at the shop. Not to mention her history in South Burrow.

I opened the front door and let Willow out to do her business. She trotted straight for Jim, who was unloading some equipment to be stored in the barn.

"Hey, Jim." I waved to him, but he didn't hear me. I yelled louder, "Hi, Jim!"

He turned once Willow was around his ankles. He bent down to pat her and then waved to me. I walked over to get her. Once you'd given her a good belly rub, it was hard to get rid of her.

"I'm sorry. Did I wake you?" Jim asked.

Ginger had told me that Jim usually waits until after he thinks I'm up before he goes to the barn, since he can make so much noise in the barn.

"Nah, I accidently overslept, but Marlene is opening for me today." I brushed my bangs out of my eyes. "Did you tell Noah about Sean's truck?"

I knew he couldn't lie because he was the only person who knew.

"Holly, what did you expect me to do?" Jim's voice was inflamed and belligerent. "It's obvious that Sean murdered my brother-in-law, and I want him found. So does Ginger."

"I know." I bit my lip and looked away.

I didn't really know, but I did know that I had to watch what I said around anyone, especially Jim. The last person I wanted another visit from was Noah Druck.

"Anyway, I've gotta go." I pretended like I had a treat between my fingers. "Come on Willow."

Week, week, week, she squealed the entire way back to the cottage, her hind hooves dancing to get a sniff at my fingers.

"Holly." Jim called out. "You should stop by and see Ginger. She could use some company."

He was right. Ginger had made herself scarce over the past few days. I figured she was dealing with the loss of Doug and trying to settle his business dealings.

I threw on a jogging suit and ran a brush through my hair. It was time to face Marlene and get some answers that I desperately needed.

"You stay here." I gave Willow a pat on the head before I gathered my stuff.

Willow was scared of Marlene, and if she decided to yell at me for my line of questioning, it might make Willow a nervous wreck. And nothing good comes from a nervous piggy.

The scrap piece of paper with Donovan's number was on the counter next to my keys. I grabbed them and my new ePhone, and then I shut and locked the door behind me.

Someone had been in my house and planted Sean's cell in *The Under* of my futon. It was time I learned how to defend myself.

Pulling out of my driveway, I made a quick call to Donovan.

"Hey, Holly." Donovan sounded happy to hear from me. "Are you calling to take me up on my offer?"

"Yes," I confirmed. "Do you think you could stop by tonight?"

We agreed on a time and I gave him my address.

"I'm looking forward to it," Donovan said before he hung up.

I was looking forward to seeing him again. I was even more interested in feeling safe in my own home, and learning moves that could possibly save my life.

I pulled up in front on The Beaded Dragonfly and noticed the sign on the door was turned to display the closed side.

The two nosey women from the pier were looking in the windows.

Where in the hell was Marlene?

I got out of my car and slammed the door.

The two women jumped and turned around. Startled, they grabbed each other and took off down the sidewalk.

"Stop right there!" I screamed, and my keys were strategically placed in between my fingers like Donovan had taught me in the first defense class.

I was *so* aware of my surroundings that it wasn't even funny. As a matter of fact, I was proud of myself.

The two women stopped. There was a look of fear in their eyes.

"You two aren't going anywhere." I pointed my keys at them, and then motioned them over to the shop door. "I've got a few questions for you two."

They clutched their purses, and walked backwards up the steps. They planted their backsides up against the shop door.

I unlocked the door and ushered them in. They shuffled to one of the tables and then eased themselves down in chairs.

I looked around, but Marlene was nowhere to be seen. She hadn't even been there.

"Damn, Marlene." I muttered before I turned my attention back to the women.

"I agree." One of them muttered back.

"I second that!" The other one screamed and smacked her hand on the table.

"What?" I jumped, and held my hand over heart.

I was aware of my surroundings, but not prepared to be scared out of my skin.

"Where is Marlene?" She questioned me. "We aren't playing games anymore. Are we Tallulah?"

Tallulah shook her head. "No, we aren't."

"That's right." The other woman stood up and put her hands on her thick hips. "I want my Spinel back. I'm going to get it one way or another."

"*Your Spinel*?" I asked, my nerves tensing immediately. "You mean the Spinel Marlene's husband gave her?"

The two women cackled.

"Husband?" Tallulah hit the other one on the arm. "Did you hear that, Mimi?"

Mimi shook her head. "I see she's lied to you too." Her lips were thin with anger.

Tallulah stood up and pulled out the empty chair next to hers. "I think you are going to need to sit down."

I think she was right.

"Marlene, precious Marlene is a gold digger." Mimi said, with a fire in her eyes. "She pretends to love them on their deathbeds, takes their money, and then disappears."

"Mmm hmm, that's right." Tallulah was the best head nodder I'd ever seen.

"You see, she began to date my husband while we were separated, but he was still my husband." Mimi planted her elbows on the table and leaned in. "On his death bed, she took his Spinel, which was a family heirloom. When his mother died, she left it to me."

She sat back and crossed her arms.

"That yellow Spinel was locked away in a safety deposit box. Marlene flashed them the key, and without any identification, they let her in." Mimi stood up and paced back and forth as she continued her story.

"The bank video tapes proved it." Tallulah took the chance to have her say between Mimi catching her breath.

"We've been looking all over for her. Then we saw your newspaper article in the South Burrow Daily about the new shop." Mimi said.

I snapped my fingers. "I remember the picture they took had Marlene in it." I pointed over to the cash register where I had taped the picture on the side of it.

"That's when we started coming around here. But she refuses to talk to us." Mimi's nostrils flared with fury.

Everything started clicking. Marlene being so secretive about her past, her obsession with learning the wrapping bead technique, plus her interest in Doug Sloan.

"We left her several notes." Tallulah said. "Finally she did meet us at the pier, but she refused to give it back."

"We were going to give her one last chance when we came in yesterday." Mimi sat back down and pounded her fist on the table. "But she refused to listen and kicked us out of the shop. I'd love to take one of those four-inch heels of hers and whack her with it."

"What? Here? You were here with Marlene yesterday?" I was more confused than ever.

"Yes, we came in here to talk to her, but she refused to listen." Mimi drew back in the chair.

"Oh, and that camera man asked us to leave. He said we were disturbing the business." Tallulah seemed inexplicably dissatisfied.

Mimi sat still looking into the distance as if she was trying to remember something.

Jim did say he was going to come and readjust the cameras, but he'd failed to mention that he was here, or anything about the little scuffle.

"Anyway, that nice handyman was going to say something, but we haven't heard from him either." Tallulah reminded Mimi.

"That's right. We haven't heard from him." Mimi confirmed.

"Sean? You've seen Sean?" This discovery hit me full force. I steadied myself against the table.

Had he been here all along? Why was he having these conversations with Marlene? What did he want to tell me about Marlene?

"A few days ago, when we came in here, he was standing right there." Mimi pointed to the counter where I've seen him lean over to take in Marlene in all her glory. Only, I didn't have to worry about Marlene wanting Sean. He was too poor for her taste.

"He said he'd find out and he took our number," Mimi said.

Frantically, I shook my head. "Marlene was supposed to be here and Sean"…I fumbled around the shop…"Sean won't return my calls."

I took their phone numbers and hurried them out of the shop before the beading class arrived.

Chapter Twenty-Seven

There were so many things I needed to do before the beading class started, but couldn't think about even attempting to do a single one of them. Tallulah and Mimi didn't help matters. They've confused me even more.

The front door opened, Cheri popped her head in. "I wanted to say hi before class."

He-hon, he-hon, he-hon. Willow pulled her head out of a trashcan underneath one of the beading tables. She darted out to greet Cheri, tipping over the can and spilling the trash onto the floor. Great, another mess for me to clean up.

"You're such a good girl," Cheri said, bending down to pet her. In typical Willow style, she rolled over onto her back with her little piggy hooves in the air waiting for Cheri to scratch her belly. "Can I take her for a quick walk before class?"

"Yes," I answered quickly before she decided to change her mind.

That would be one thing that I could cross off my to-do list, even though taking Willow for a walk was probably the healthiest chore on the list.

"Okay." Cheri walked over to the counter where I kept Willow's leash." Let's go, beautiful."

Groink, groink, groink. Willow's little black eyes were fixed on Cheri and her tail twirled in excitement.

I walked them to the door and flipped the sign to open.

The storage room is where I store everyone's projects out of the way. I gathered up the projects for that night's group. The class was one of the more advanced classes I taught. It covered the techniques of using wire, wrapping, and making flat looped spirals which made this earring project very popular. It was a difficult project that required the use of both hands, so I only had five students per table, giving them plenty of elbowroom.

I also limited the class to only ten students. That allowed me enough time to walk around to each one and give them the attention they had paid for. Each student was so different. That was the best part. I enjoyed helping them learn.

Just then, the shop phone rang.

"The Beaded Dragonfly," I said into the cordless on my way back into the storage room to get the snacks for the class.

"Holly?" Jim Rush's voice escalated as if he was surprised I answered. "You're still there? Aren't you closed?" Why would Jim think I was closed? Is it a weekend?

I laughed. Of all people, Jim should know that a business owner just doesn't shut the lights off at quitting time.

"Why are you calling me if you didn't think I would answer?"

"I was going to run by on my way home, and readjust the camera angles for you," he said. "Ginger said I should call first, because you might have a class scheduled. She said that you probably wouldn't want me making noise if you did."

I put out a few cookies and chips, along with some two-liter bottles of soft drinks on the open bead tables. I had to make sure it was back far enough so Willow couldn't stick her big snout up and get into it.

"Ginger was right." There was no way I wanted to see Jim Rush on a ladder during a beading class, though it was important to get those cameras working as soon as possible. "We'll be out of here within one-and-a-half hours if you can stop by after that."

The phone was between my ear and shoulder, which was not comfortable. I'm surprised Flora's head wasn't permanently lying to the side, and her shoulder hunched up. Regardless, it was the only way to talk to Jim while I got out the chain-nose and round-nose pliers the students were going to need.

"Sounds good. I'll be there."

"Oh, Jim," I said, stopping him from hanging up. "How's Ginger doing?"

I was very concerned about Ginger. She always remained poised in crisis situations and put on a brave face. But with Doug's murder, she'd been lying low, not coming to any Diva meetings or even returning my calls.

"She's not doing so well. Even though we weren't that close to Doug, he really was all the family she had left." He sighed. "She's got a lot of stuff on her plate, being the only Sloan left in Swanee. Anyway, I'll be by later."

After Jim hung up, I had just enough time to get out the rest of the supplies they'd need to make the earrings; ear pins, the jump rings, 20 gauge wire, and all the beads.

The Miss U Heart Pendant that would dangle from the earrings when the project was finished was so simple and elegant. I had three colors to choose from, light pink, hot pink, and red. Personally, the red one was my favorite.

I touched my ear, feeling the ones I had made last night so I could show the students the finished project.

One by one, the class trickled in. They each picked out a Miss U Heart Pendant and took a seat. Weeks before, we had been going over all the separate techniques to make the earrings, but tonight it was time to put those techniques together.

"Okay, let's get started." I herded everyone to their tables after they had mingled around the snack table and socialized for a few minutes."

I went over every single element and stone on their bead boards, reassuring them that they were going to love putting together all the steps they'd learned so far.

"Cut a 5-1/2 inch length of jeweler's wire." I used the flush-cutter pliers to cut my wire. "Form a 5-loop flat spiral on one end of the wire."

I demonstrated the technique and then walked around to make sure they were doing it correctly. A few times, I had to stop and help form the spiral, since it was a difficult technique for even a beading expert.

"Bend the straight end of the wire so it passes through the center of one 17mm Swarovski Miss U Heart drop, and back through the center of the flat wire spiral." I slipped on a light pink heart this time, since I was wearing the red pair.

I love making the project alongside the students. It shows them that I know what I'm doing, plus, anything I make in class goes into the glass counter to be sold. I sold a lot of premade jewelry for customers looking for quick gifts.

"String three 4mm Swarovski bicone beads onto the straight end of the wire." I picked up the beads and strung them. "Form a simple loop on the straight end of the wire."

The best part about that project was the simple easy steps. The techniques were hard to learn, but once they had them down, the earrings were a breeze to make.

"Open a 4mm round gold-plated jumpring and pass it through the simple loop formed in Step 3 and the loop on a gold-plated kidney earwire. Close the jumpring." I held the finished dangling earring up to show them what I meant.

A few of them needed help trying to hold pliers in one hand and the earring in the other without dropping it. Once everyone was finished with the first earring, I left them alone to make the second one on their own.

It was perfect time for me to finish Margaret McGee's necklace. It was turning out to be more stunning than it looked when it was laid out in her hand. The 4MM pink Swarovski reflected off the 2MM sterling silver balls. The Lotus Pearls added elegance to the entire piece.

"That's beautiful." Cheri gently touched the necklace as I finished the final crimp.

"I think so too." I held it up to take a good look. "I hope the bride likes it."

I frowned after I laid it back on the table. The satisfaction I thought I was going to have finishing up my first client's order wasn't as great as I thought it was going to be.

"Are you okay? Cheri asked, touching my arm.

"I'm fine." I've never been good at disguising my feelings. I looked around to make sure no one was listening, leaned over, and whispered, "I've always wanted to design for clients and now that I have one, I can't enjoy it because of the murder and all."

Margaret's necklace was almost complete. I took the white polishing cloth and cleaned each element, making it shine before I put it in the black velvet jewelry pouch.

"It's going to all work out." Cheri went back to her earrings.

I checked on the other students to make sure they were okay, and they were all doing fine. Some were actually starting on a second pair because they liked them so much. Some of them were planning to give them away as gifts. It made me happy to think that one of my designs was liked by so many members of the class.

There was enough time for me to finish the bridesmaid's bracelets before class was over. I had to hurry up and get this order done before Margaret changed her mind and wanted to cancel our contract. Her mother still didn't seem so sure about letting me do the wedding with the murder and all. Plus, Margaret's dad was the city attorney, as well as the Sloan's private lawyer.

Also, getting paid would be good. Since Sean was nowhere to be found, I was sure my alimony check wasn't in the mail. And rent on The Beaded Dragonfly was due… to the Sloan's.

Chapter Twenty-Eight

The next morning was the time to visit Ginger and see if Jim was there. I needed him to get me the video footage of what he had of the shop. I needed to see Mimi and Tallulah talking to Marlene, and Sean talking to Marlene. Maybe there would be a clue.

Sean's voice message played in my head.

Damn machine. I wished I could recover that tape. Sean knew something about Marlene and he wanted to tell me.

I gasped.

Marlene had been trying to get her claws into Doug, and maybe Sean overheard something between Doug and Marlene the night Doug was murdered at The Livin' End. According to Mimi and Tallulah, Marlene would do anything for money. Would she be willing to murder for it?

Hopefully, Jim got the camera angles perfect when he came back last night to The Beaded Dragonfly. Even though the video angles weren't exactly perfect when Sean was in there, and it wouldn't have volume, I would be able to read Sean's body language.

I pulled up next to the curb in front of Ginger's house. I didn't want to pull into the driveway and block anyone in, just in case someone was giving their condolences. All of the curtains were pulled in the front windows. Ginger must have been worse off than we Divas thought.

I knocked a couple of times but no one answered. I walked around the side of the house and didn't see Jim's truck.

I was a little disappointed, because I really wanted to talk to him about the video. I went ahead and stepped onto the back porch and looked in the back window.

Sometimes, Ginger liked to sit at the kitchen table and work on the Sudoku puzzle from the morning paper while watching her afternoon soap operas.

On several occasions, I'd told her she was beginning to act like an old woman, even though she was only in her forties.

I looked as far as I could see and she wasn't in there, but the TV was on.

I walked back to the front of the house, but stopped when my ePhone vibrated.

Hoping it was Sean, I pulled it out of my pocket. It was Bernadine, the only other person who knew I had a cell.

"Hey, Bernadine. Can I call you back in a few?" I asked in a hushed whisper.

I didn't want Ginger to overhear me.

"Marlene is back at your cottage." Bernadine gasped, causing a shiver of panic to run down my spine.

"See what she's doing," I told he, then bent down behind the bushes that ran along Ginger's house when I heard a car driving by.

I didn't want anyone in Swanee to know I had a cell phone. It would spread like wildfire if even one person found out.

"How do you expect me to do that?" Bernadine asked with an unwelcome frankness.

I covered my mouth with my hand and said, "If you can see her, you must be near my house."

There was no way Bernadine could see clear across the lake from her house.

"I'm looking through my binoculars. I saw movement and I thought it was you." She took a deep breath. "I was going to see if you wanted to walk, but then I thought it might be Jim in the barn."

"What is she doing?" I asked, wondering if she was the one who planted Sean's cell phone in my futon.

She kidnapped him, took his cell, and put it in my house to frame me. Only she didn't know that I'd never put anything in an *Under.*

"I don't know. I just saw her turn the corner of your house, and then I called you." Bernadine was sucking in air.

"What are you doing?" I asked. The last thing I needed was Bernadine having a heart attack on me. "Dishes?"

There was clanking in the background and some water splashing like she was doing dishes, but I knew better. Bernadine never did dishes, nor would she get those fancy manicured nails in dirty dishwater.

"I'm rowing to your side of the lake to see what Marlene is doing, like you asked." Bernadine said. "I've got to go. Come home, now."

"Holly?" I heard Ginger calling my name coming from the front of the house. "Holly?"

I slipped the phone back in my pocket and came out from behind the bush. Luckily, Ginger hadn't seen me.

"Hi." I shot around the corner of the house and hopped up on the front porch. "I was just knocking on your back door."

She held the door open for me to come in.

"I was walking by the door and saw your car parked out front." She said, hugged me tightly, and then held me out at arm's length. "I didn't hear you knock. Are you losing weight?"

I stepped back and ran my hands along my waist. "I'm working on it. Can you really tell?"

"I can." She nodded and smiled.

It was good to see Ginger smile. She looked almost normal, but I knew that wasn't the case.

"I wanted to stop by since I haven't seen or heard from you. We've missed you at the Divas meetings." I reached out and squeezed her arm.

"I know. It's just so hard, knowing that someone would really kill my brother." Her expression grew serious.

"Well, I have to run." I tapped my watch.

I really needed to get home and catch Marlene red-handed, or follow her to see where she's going.

"Can't you stay for a minute?" Ginger nervously rubbed her hands together. "I just don't understand why you wouldn't call the police after Sean skipped town."

"I know what it looks like, but I honestly don't think Sean could have killed Doug." I had to be honest with my best friend, but not too honest.

"I think Sean knows something. Maybe he didn't do it, but Holly, it seems awfully suspicious." Ginger's eyes looked tired. She wasn't dolled up in her scarves like she usually was. "Plus, everyone in town is scared to death."

That was true. Jim had been super busy installing cameras in everyone's homes.

"Jim has been working overtime to help ease people's fear." Ginger dabbed her eyes with a tissue. "We haven't had a moment to even grieve."

"Oh, Ginger." I hugged my dear friend, and snuck a quick glance at my watch.

I pictured Bernadine taking an oar to Marlene's head.

"Let's get the Divas together and have some girl time." I said, and she agreed.

"Is Jim here?" I asked, just in case he was.

"No." Ginger sighed deeply. "He's installing more cameras."

"Do you know where he keeps the video of the shop footage?" I didn't want to seem too obvious why I'd really stopped by. "I think one of the teenagers might have swiped some Bali beads when I wasn't looking."

I lied. Again.

"Just stop by the hardware store and Joni can help you out." Ginger leaned up against the door, holding it open.

"Joni?" I was curious to why the cashier at Sloan Hardware was handling the video footage.

"She needed extra hours, so we have her labeling the tapes and switching them out."

I tucked that information in the back of my head. This was perfect. I'd make sure Jim wasn't there when I stopped by to see Joni. That way, he wouldn't run straight to Noah.

Chapter Twenty-Nine

I drove as fast as I could to get home, only to find Bernadine one side of the front porch with an oar and Donovan on the other side.

Donovan. I had completely forgotten about our little meeting.

"Where have you been?" Bernadine raised her eyebrows and tilted her head toward Donovan.

"Hi, Donovan." I smiled at both of them. "After last night, I decided I could use some one-on-one defense classes."

Bernadine had already forgotten about Marlene, and why she rowed over to my side of the lake.

"I bet you do." She looked Donovan up and down, and I couldn't help but look too.

He looked much better in his jeans, thermal tee, and Puma shoes. He also wasn't all sweaty like he was in defense class at The Moose.

"You're looking awfully nice to be demonstrating defense positions." Bernadine was grinning from ear to ear talking to Donovan. She flung her crimson hair behind her shoulder. "I'd be more than happy to be Holly's partner again."

"Oh, that's okay." I took her by the shoulders and pointed her in the direction of her rowboat. "I'll call you later."

"I know you will." She waved over her shoulder. "Remember, I have binoculars."

"I'll be right back." I told Donovan, and then jogged down to the lakeshore. "Quick, what happened to Marlene?"

Bernadine looked over my shoulder at Donovan and then back at me. "She was gone by the time I got over here."

My eyebrows drew together in confusion.

"Yeah, weird." Bernadine got in her rowboat, paused, and pointed to Donovan. "Can I tell the Divas about this?"

"No! This is just between you and me." I gestured between us. "Besides, I've got to tell you about today. I'll call you later."

I stood at the edge of the water until Bernadine got halfway across the lake. I turned around and walked back up to the cottage where Donovan was still standing on my porch.

"I'm sorry about that." I motioned toward Bernadine. "She and I walk every day, and I lost track of time."

I unlocked the door and gave the bottom corner a swift kick like I always did, but the door flew open without the help of my foot. I teetered back and forth before Donovan put his arms around me to help me with my balance.

"Are you okay?" He laughed out loud.

I surveyed the door. I shut it and then opened it again. The bottom corner was not sticking like it always had.

"Strange." I pointed out the corner. "I've always had to kick the bottom of the door to open it."

"It could be the weather. Wood contracts when the weather changes," Donovan said and then stepped into the cottage.

He-hon, he-hon, he-hon, Willow was delighted with a new pair of shoes to sniff.

"You have a pet pig?" His surprise was obviously genuine, judging by the expression on his face.

"Doesn't everyone?" I questioned him jokingly.

I probably should've warned him that I had a pet pig before I invited him over, but it never crossed my mind.

"What made you decide to get a pig as a pet?" Donovan laughed when Willow plopped down on the floor in front of him and rolled over with her hooves sticking up in the air.

He surprised me by giving her a good belly scratch.

"Oh, you've done it now." I bent down, giving her my own little rub. "My ex-husband, Sean, always wanted a pet pig. Right before our divorce, he went out and bought Willow without me knowing. The only problem was, a couple days later, he decided he didn't want a pet pig or a wife either."

Memories like those should make me happy that Sean was missing, but they didn't help ease my worried mind. Even though he was a jerk, he used to be *my* jerk, and those feelings hadn't disappeared along with Sean.

"I think you got the good end of the deal." Donovan looked into my eyes and then gave an irresistibly devastating grin.

"Let's get started, shall we?" I jumped to my feet and pulled my shirt hem down over my waistband.

"Cheri told me that your shop had been broken into." Donovan arms hung to the ground as he bent over to stretch. "I'm glad she wasn't home when it happened."

I was glad too. If I'm scared to death here, I knew Cheri had to be freaked out living above the shop.

As Donovan stretched, I followed suit and wondered why we did this before class. There was no way I would say to the attacker, "could you wait for a second while I stretch out so I can be sure to be limber enough to be able to use the moves I learned in self-defense class against you?"

Despite that, I continued to mimic Donovan.

"It's been broken into twice," I said, referring to the shop while I raised my hands way above my head and leaned over to the right. "I hope the camera stickers in the shop windows deter any more break-ins."

It was perfectly clear that the shop break-ins weren't just any old break-in. Someone was after me. Just a thought, but wouldn't he or she have to think it was the two ladies trying to get the Spinel who broke into the shop?

"Cool! I haven't seen one of these in years." Donovan was clearly amused when he saw my old answering machine.

"Oh, that." I switched sides and leaned to the left. "It was working, but the tape is all bundled up around the little turn thingies."

If only…I wondered about the message on the jumbled mess that held the answers to what Sean was saying about Marlene.

Donovan opened the cover, exposing the tape.

"Stop! Don't touch that." I ran over there and slammed the lid shut. I couldn't risk compromising what little tape remained that I might be able to save.

"I was just going to see if I could fix it for you." He pointed to the machine.

"It's fine. Don't worry about it." I gestured him back over to the center of the room so we could get started. "You're here to teach me self-defense, not to fix my broken answering machine."

"I love fooling with old electronics. I bet I could have it back to you in a couple of days, tape and all." He said.

"Really?" A soft gasp escaped my lips.

Maybe I should let him try. I was no closer to finding out what was on the tape, and Donovan might be able to fix it. I could finally find out the missing link to where Marlene was hiding Sean. If she was, in fact, hiding Sean.

"What do you say we do some basic self defense moves, I take you to dinner, and then I'll take the machine home to work on it?" He asked with determination.

"Deal." I stuck my hand out, wondering why I had agreed to go to dinner with him, but I was definitely hoping he could fix the tape.

"Okay, let's get started." He rubbed his hands together. "The main thing to know about self-defense is that you can use various parts of your body as powerful weapons to fight against attackers."

I stood in awe as he made some pretty cool moves with his arms.

"Being aware of your surroundings is the first step to not get attacked." There was defiance in his tone as well as a subtle challenge. "If you do get attacked, you need to repeat, 'confuse, leave.'"

This was beginning to seem a little silly to me.

"Repeat after me, Confuse. Leave." His voice rang with command. He nodded towards me to mimic him. "Confuse. Leave."

"Confuse. Leave." I said, half-heartedly.

"I'm serious, Holly." His voice was calm and his gaze was steady. "Why am I here if you aren't going to try to learn protect yourself?"

"I'm sorry." I lowered my head in shame at his brow beating, and then I screamed, "Confuse! Leave!"

"Good. Now I'm going to show you three basic defense techniques that will help you in any situation." He pointed to his noggin'. "You have to remember them, and not freak out while you are being attacked."

These moves were designed to allow you to escape and flee from the attacker. These moves included head butting, getting out of a wristlock, and shin kicking.

The V-Trigger is used when you are being grabbed by the arm, wrist, or hand and your other hand is free.

"Make a tight fist." Donovan held his fist up in the air, and then he pointed to the V formed by the first and second fingers close to the knuckle. "You need to hit that spot on the attacker's hand with the knuckle of your free hand."

I did exactly what he told me as he pretended to be my attacker by holding my wrist.

"Good. Now turn around, yell, and run."

I screamed, "Confuse! Leave!" and ran down the hall. I could hear Willow squeal from fright in the bedroom.

"You don't yell 'confuse, leave' when you are being attacked. Just yell to draw attention to yourself." He was laughing hysterically.

"What do you do if your attacker is wearing gloves?" Donovan pulled some gloves out of his jean pockets, and put them on.

"No clue. That's why you're here." I danced on my tiptoes like Rocky.

I was feeling pretty good and pumped up.

"The V-Trigger isn't going to work if your attacker has these on." He held his gloved hands in the air. "So we need to learn to use a different part of your body."

Donovan grabbed me by both my hands to show me one way that I could be attacked. He gestured for me to take his wrists as if I was the assailant.

"You are going to use the Shin Insertion method. Drag your foot up at a 45-degree angle to get your toe up and into the shin, as if you were doing a high-step walk." He demonstrated and looked like he was marching rather than walking. "Generate as much force as possible. Kick until the attacker lets go."

He pretended to kick me. When I let go, he screamed and ran down the hall. He didn't come back. I looked to see where he'd gone, and he came strolling out with Willow in his arms.

"I think we're scaring her." He let her give him piggy kisses. "Do you think you can remember those two basic moves?"

I made some of the motions in the air. "I do," I said with confidence.

It did make me feel a little bit more confident and safe.

"These are moves you should practice on a daily basis." He put Willow down on the futon and made the motions as he said them. "The V-Trigger is just like knocking on a door, and the Shin Insertion is like marching. There is no need to build muscle or learn karate." I erased the last part because I didn't know what it meant.

I punched the air while high stepping around the room.

Donovan wiped the sweat from his brow. "I think you can remember those moves."

I nodded. I might not be able to remember the exact moves, but I could remember the parts that would hurt Marlene. . .I mean my attacker.

"Good. I'm starving. Let's go get some grub." He patted his belly.

Suddenly, it occurred to me that Marlene was the only other person who had a key to my shop. She was the last person I wanted in there.

"You ready to go?" Donovan asked.

I put my hand up to my head and bent over. "Thank you, but I'm going to have to pass. I just got the worse headache."

I really did enjoy his company and wouldn't mind going out to dinner under different circumstances, but I had to get my key back from Marlene and fast.

"Working out really hard can do that to you. Be sure to drink plenty of fluids during the day and especially after practicing like we did just now." He said and picked up the answering machine. "I'm expecting a rain check on dinner though."

"Definitely." I held the door open for him.

Donovan gave Willow one last rub before she snorted off down the hall.

Chapter Thirty

I tossed and turned all night long. I gave up and got out of bed when I realized I wasn't going to get any sleep until I knew that Sean was safe and sound and Marlene was behind bars. Well, if Marlene was behind it.

It was almost time to get up anyway, so I let Willow out. Bernadine's house was still dark, which wasn't unusual because she was a late sleeper.

I practiced a couple quick self-defense moves so I wouldn't forget what I had learned while Willow was out doing her business. I let her in as soon as she scratched at the door and she darted straight for the futon. Instead of jumping on it, she slid, hooves out, butt in air, and squealed like I've never heard her squeal before.

"Willow!" I bent down next to her, and clapped my hands. "Get out of there now."

This pig was acting all sorts of strange lately. I poked her butt because it was the only body part sticking out from *The Under*, only it made her squeal louder.

"Willow?" I put my hands on her butt, and tried to pull her out, but she was stuck. "Willow?"

The poor pink thing was becoming a nervous piggy. Her back hooves were clawing the hardwood trying to free her, but she wasn't budging.

I got on one side of the futon and gripped the armrest. I had to lift up my side enough so she could get out. On a wing and a prayer, I hoisted my end up, Willow flew out and ran straight back to the bedroom.

I put the futon down, wondering what was under it that would make Willow dive for it. I lay on the floor to see what it was. I squinted. I couldn't see anything. The dark *Under* wasn't going to deliver the goods without a fight.

"I'm going to win this." I pointed to myself like *The Under* could really hear me.

I went into the kitchen to retrieve the plug-in flashlight that I took from Sean, and clicked it on to make sure it worked.

"Aha!" I pointed the light toward the futon and waved it around like a light saber.

I lay back down on the floor and the light illuminated the dark *Under*. Just a glimmer of pink was visible. I zeroed in on the glistening hot pink spot.

There was no way I was going to move the futon or stick my hand in *The Under*, but I could get the broom. I jabbed with the handle and knocked the pink thing out.

I crawled on my knees to see what it was.

A fingernail?

"What the hell?" I inspected it more closely.

It was a hot pink press-on nail. There was only one person I knew that was fake all the way to the tippy tops of her eyelashes.

Marlene.

Here was my proof that Marlene planted that cell phone. At least it was proof enough for me. I took it into the kitchen and put it in a snack baggie. Willow came running back out because she thought I was giving her a snack.

"You are one smart piggy." I dangled the zip lock over her head to show her the evidence she found. I put it on top of my refrigerator. "I will put this up here until I can gather all the evidence I need."

There were a couple of stops I needed to make before I went to work. The Beaded Dragonfly's mortgage wasn't going to pay for itself. Today was the first day of Beading 101, and I couldn't afford to be closed another day.

Before Willow and I headed out, I glanced across the lake to see if Bernadine's kitchen light was on. Before I went to work, I'd usually see a few lights on, but not that day.

I called her anyway. If I woke her, I didn't care. She'd offended my slumber plenty of times. I wanted to give her a quick rundown of what was going on.

Besides, it was in the Divas creed that we could call anytime of the day, and it didn't matter what we were doing.

Unfortunately, she didn't answer, so I was going to have to leave a message.

"Hey, Bernadine. I know you are coming to the bead class today, and I'll see you there, but I wanted to give you a heads-up on what I think has really happened to Sean. Marlene is the one who planted Sean's cell under my futon."

I went on to explain how Willow was ass-end up in *The Under* of the futon with a hot pink fiberglass nail teasing her. And reminded her that Marlene was the only one in Swanee that wore hot pink fiberglass nails on a daily basis.

Coincidence?

I think not.

"Anyway, I've got more digging to do, but I'll fill you in on those details later." I said my goodbyes and hung up.

If she had trouble following me, I'm sure she'd call my new ePhone.

Willow danced around the floor under where her leash was hanging and twirled her tail. There was no way I could leave her here again. Plus, I didn't want to come home to roast pork like the bunny that Glenn Close's character boiled in Fatal Attraction.

With a click of the leash, and another quick glance over at Bernadine's dark house, Willow and I were on our way to our first stop---the Swanee Police station.

Since Noah Druck was true to his word, he'd already be in South Burrow. I bet he'd already impounded Sean's truck if it hadn't been sold to someone else yet.

Willow and I walked right in like we always did and the officers fed her pieces of their leftover doughnuts.

"What can we do for you, miss?" One of the new deputies asked from behind the counter.

Noah's desk was empty like I'd hoped it would be.

"Is Noah around?" I pretended to look around to throw him off.

"He's gone for the day to a neighboring town." The officer tugged on his belt. "I'm in charge today."

I bet you are. I smiled, knowing this new guy probably had no clue how close-knit Swanee was.

"Is that right?" I batted my eyelashes, but they got caught on the edges of my bangs. "I'm here to get my police report about the break-in at my shop. I need to turn it into my insurance company."

"What's the name?" He picked up a cardboard box with a bunch of papers in it.

"Holly Harper from The Beaded Dragonfly." I folded my hands and Willow sat down next to my feet.

"Wow. You're the Holly Harper that all the talk is about around here?" His eyes grew wide as I nodded. "Well, I'll be. Yep, lots of talk about you."

"I bet there is." I noticed his badge said Gilley. I tapped my watch and said, "Officer Gilley, I've got to get back to the shop, if you wouldn't mind grabbing that report so I can get out of your hair."

"Yes, ma'am." He scurried to the back and through a door.

"Stay." I held my hand out to Willow and hurried over to Noah's desk.

Sean's cell had to be there somewhere. I had to check his call log. Someone, probably Marlene, knew that Noah was going to be at my house that night, and she wanted him to find the phone, so she called it.

Luck was on my side, because the cell was in the second drawer I checked, as if it had been waiting on me.

"Hello, old friend." I scrolled through it like I had so many times before when I was looking for other women's numbers.

The time stamp gave me the exact number that I needed. I grabbed a pen and scrap paper off Noah's desk and scribbled the number on it. I put the cell back in the drawer, grabbed Willow, and bolted out the door.

There was no time to wait for the police report. I had to get to my next stop before the shop opened. Sloan's Hardware.

Chapter Thirty-One

I drove around the lot a couple of times to see if Jim's truck was there. I didn't see it, so I thought I'd take my chance to find Joni.

If he was there, I could hire him to change the locks at the bead shop.

It was early in the morning, so there was barely anyone in the store. I found my way to customer service where Joni was sitting underneath a sign that read, "Rush Protection Service."

"Hi, Holly. You here to see Jim?" Joni folded her hands in front of her and sat them on the counter.

"Yes. I need some of the video footage of my shop." Oh, how I prayed Jim wasn't in the back.

"I'm sorry. He isn't here, but I'd be more than happy to help." Joni jumped off the stool in excitement. "They promoted me."

Her five-foot frame padded around the Customer Service counter, and she motioned for me to follow her.

"I heard." I boasted, trying to inflate her ego. "Ginger said that you've been working really hard."

Joni jumped up and clapped her hands in delight. "Really? I *have* been working hard. I really want to make them proud."

"Oh, you do." I nodded.

Joni unlocked the door just before her name was called over the loud speaker.

"I'll be right back. Go in and help yourself. I have alphabetized all the tapes." Joni flung the door open, and walked up to the front of the hardware shop.

I stood in awe, looking at rows and rows of VCR tapes on steel shelves. Who still uses VCR tapes? I started at the A's and ran my finger along the videos until I reached the B's.

Ginger wasn't kidding when she said that everyone and their brother in Swanee wanted a security camera.

We might not know who the killer was, but I did know that this had to be filling Ginger's pockets, which were pretty well padded before.

"Beaded Dragonfly, The." I said, touching each 'The' tape there was. "Tan Your Hide, The; End of the Line Liquor, The; Livin' End, The."

But nothing labeled The Beaded Dragonfly. There definitely wasn't one for the shop. On second thought, Jim did say that it would take a few days to fill a tape since we were only taping during the hours the shop was closed. Maybe there wasn't a full tape yet since it only had been a couple of days since he'd installed them.

I just needed to find out which recording device the camera feed was sent to. That's what I get for opting for the cheaper package. Jim did try to talk me into having the monitors located at the shop, but I refused.

Hindsight, I sighed.

Before I left, I did one more check through the "The's." Gently, I pulled out the cassettes for The Livin' End. I tried to recall where the cameras were in the smoky and dimly-lit bar. I couldn't remember seeing any.

What if there were some clues on these tapes? I was desperate for anything.

I tucked them under my arm and walked out of the store. Joni was too busy helping a customer to even notice me. I slipped out unseen.

Willow was asleep in the passenger seat like a good little piggy. I put the cassettes on the floorboard.

"One quick drive by The Livin' End, and then on to the shop." I scratched Willow's ears and got a satisfied snort in return.

The gravel parking lot was empty. Slowly, I pulled in to see if I could find any outside cameras. I scanned the outside of the building twice and came up empty handed. I drove around the light post and happened to look up.

There it was. There was a sphere that sure did look like a Rush Protection Service outdoor camera.

"We've got something," I said to Willow and put the pedal to the metal.

I picked up my phone to call Sean and tell him I knew something was wrong, but put the phone down. His phone was in Noah's desk and did me no good.

Chapter Thirty-Two

It was already after ten when we pulled up in front of the shop. Some of the class members were standing next to the door, including Flora.

"I'm sorry I'm late." I profusely apologized and unlocked the door.

"Where is everyone?" Flora twirled a strand of her wavy brown hair with one hand and held the phone against her ear with the other.

"I have no idea where the Divas are," I said, and quickly got the bead boards and a few supplies out for the class. "I left Bernadine a message on her machine, but I haven't heard from her."

In this class, I was going to teach the group how to start a simple beaded bracelet. Crimping was first on the list, since it was how the toggle stayed on.

"Of course you haven't. You don't have a cell for anyone to get in touch with you." Flora held her cell out for me to see.

If only she knew. I couldn't tell her I had the new ePhone. The fewer people that knew, the better.

Before class, I went into my office and called Donovan.

"Hi, Holly." He answered more cheerfully than I thought he would.

"Hi. I was hoping to collect on that rain check tonight." I held my breath for an answer.

"Absolutely. What time should I pick you up?" He asked.

"I was thinking that after work I could pick up a pizza and we could watch some old videos." I was technically *using* him.

I did enjoy his company, and I was sure it would have been different if it weren't under these circumstances.

He mentioned he was an old equipment guy, and how much older could you get than VCR tapes?

"Okay. What movies?" He questioned me.

"Do you have a VCR?" I felt my check flush with embarrassment for asking him that.

"Yes, but that's an odd question."

"Good. I know you're going to like what I have to show you." My voice escalated with excitement.

I had to put on a good act in order to get what I needed.

"Sounds good." He gave me his address, and we were all set.

"One more thing." I interrupted him. "Can I bring Willow?"

I never took her to anyone's house without asking first. Some people think pigs are…well, pigs. But not Willow. She's cleaner than any house pet I've ever seen.

"Of course, she's welcome here." He said, and then we hung up.

Halfway through class, Cheri burst through the door with a huge smile on her face.

I was bent over one of the students, who was sitting next to Flora, showing her how to hide the snipped piece of wire in a bead.

"Donovan told me you two have a dinner date tonight," Cheri whispered between me and Flora.

"Big deal. What's dinner?" I shrugged my shoulders.

"Defense Donovan? Dinner?" Flora hung up her cell and put it on her bead board next to the all-sterling silver 8mm bracelet she was finishing. "A very big deal."

"Yes, Defense Donovan," I said. Leave it up to the Divas to give him a nickname.

Willow must've heard Cheri. She high-tailed it as fast as her hooves could carry her to Cheri's side.

"Hey, girl." Cheri was the only Diva brave enough to actually ever pick Willow up and let her give her kisses. "You want to go for a walk?"

Willow fought her way out of Cheri's arms. She knew what 'walk' meant.

"We're just having a pizza and watching some old movies." I clicked Willow's leash on and handed it to Cheri.

"Wait until I tell the other Divas." Flora's nails were clicking away on the screen of her phone.

Yep, there were no secrets between us. Or so we thought.

Chapter Thirty-Three

The class was a huge success, but Flora was not doing well on her goal to tell the Divas about my dinner date with Defense Donovan. None of the Divas answered their phones, including Bernadine.

She even tried Marlene, and never once questioned why she wasn't at the shop. If Flora had questioned me, I'm not sure I'd have been able to keep my little investigation a secret.

Before I closed up for the night, I called the local pizzeria to order our pie and have it delivered to Donovan's house. It should be delivered by the time I got there and finished explaining my situation.

I typed Donovan's address into my fancy new ePhone. With the shop all locked up, Willow and I headed over there.

I tried calling Bernadine, but got her machine again. This didn't worry me, because it wasn't unusual for Bernadine to get a wild hair up her butt and drive to a big city just to get some shopping in. The Divas could go days without hearing from her.

I did think she would at least call me in light of everything that had transpired.

Oh, well. I shoved those thoughts to the back of my mind when we pulled up to Donovan's house. It was similar to the house Sean and I had shared, but Donovan's landscape was immaculate.

The hedges were neatly trimmed, and the edging along the sidewalk was perfect. Even the colors in the flowerbed were coordinated.

He waved from the front door before I even turned the car off. He was wearing a black tracksuit. Most of the time, I didn't like the look of a man in a sweat suit, but with his tall slender frame, he actually looked pretty good.

I grabbed the videos off the passenger floor and Willow's leash off the seat.

"Hey, you two." Donovan took the VHS tapes out of my hand, and read the label. "The Livin' End."

"Uh-huh." I followed Willow into his house.

Of course, her snout took us straight to the kitchen.

"Is it okay to let her off her leash?" I wanted to make sure he hadn't left anything out he didn't want a pig to get into. "She can be nosy."

"She's fine. Nothing here to bother." Donovan put the VHS tapes on top of his TV cabinet.

His house might resemble Sean's from the outside, but the inside had been completely remodeled to an open floor plan. He definitely didn't have the bachelor pad look with empty pizza boxes and beer bottles lying around.

The black leather motif worked with the open feel of the modern combined kitchen and family room. Granite counter tops and black cabinets added to the elegance.

"I love your house." I walked around, looking at the people in all the picture frames.

"Thanks." He handed me a cocktail. "Those are my family members."

He took a stroll down memory lane, giving me a glimpse into how each of them was related to him.

Most of his family lived two hours away. Besides being a defense instructor, he was a professor at the local community college Cheri attended. He was in the computer department.

No wonder he loved fooling around with old equipment.

Too bad my mind wasn't focused on getting a boyfriend. He would have been perfect.

"The pizza should be here any minute." I checked my watch, and then took a sip of my drink.

Not long after I said that, the doorbell rang and it was time to eat. We chatted about Swanee, my shop, and then it came time for the video portion of the evening.

"So, The Livin' End?" He picked up the tape and opened one of the doors on the TV cabinet, exposing an old VHS player. "Isn't that the name of the bar on the outskirts of town?"

"Yes." I sat down on the edge of the couch. "We are going to watch surveillance tapes of the parking lot."

There really wasn't a reason to keep the truth from him at this point. Cheri had already told him about the break-ins, and everyone knew Doug Sloan was murdered in my shop.

This was the last piece of the evidence I would collect before going to Noah. The grace period he had given me was up, and this was my Hail Mary pass. I had nothing to lose letting Donovan in on it.

He was silent as I told him about Marlene, her precious diamond, and the lack of details about her past. There was no change in his expression when I clued him in on Sean, his truck, cell phone, and the outgoing message.

"So, let me get this straight." He sat on the edge of the couch next to me. "You think that Marlene killed Doug and set Sean up. When something went wrong, she kidnapped him only to frame you. And these tapes are going to prove it?"

"Something like that." I really hoped the tapes had something on them that would prove Sean's innocence.

He circled his forefinger in the air, and said, "So, this little dinner is really about using my video equipment, not a real date."

"Something like that," I whispered, hoping that if I said it low enough that it wouldn't hurt his feelings.

"What if all this murder stuff wasn't going on? Would you go out on a date with me?" He asked. He took his finger and tilted my chin up, so he could look into my eyes.

"Yes, definitely." I nodded and smiled.

I was sure that if circumstances were different, I would definitely go out with Donovan. He might not have been my type at first sight, but he was really growing on me.

He stood up and rubbed his hands together. "Good. Let's solve this murder and exonerate you of any part of it."

We watched the tapes, pausing and rewinding often, but it wasn't until the very last tape that I saw what I needed to see.

"Wait!" I jumped up and pointed at the screen. "Rewind it."

Donovan rewound the tape and we watched it in slow motion. As plain as day, Doug followed Sean out of the bar, just like I had seen that night. I wasn't going to follow him out of The Livin' End. Ginger and I were enjoying a drink, and we weren't going to let them ruin our night.

The tape showed exactly what had transpired outside of the bar. Doug and Sean had exchanged a couple words between them, and then they did the most amazing thing. They shook hands. They were smiling the entire time.

Sean got into his truck and drove off. Doug turned around, as though he was going back into the bar, and Marlene came out of nowhere swinging. She hit Doug a couple times with her fist. He shoved her and she fell to the ground, but she got up with a vengeance. Then the tape stopped.

"What happened?" I ran over and looked at the machine.

Donovan checked a couple different things, even rewinding the last hit delivered by Marlene.

"The tape ran out." Donovan clicked a couple more buttons. The tape popped out, and it was at the end. "Is this the last video you have from there?"

"Yes. And it's all I need," I muttered, fearing that I was right.

Marlene had been the last one with Doug Sloan that night, and she had tried to frame Sean and me. Somehow, it did backfire and now she was framing me.

I grabbed my cell to call Agnes Pearl. It was clear that she might be in danger.

"Hello?" Agnes answered.

A big sigh of relief escaped my lips.

"Agnes, its Holly Harper." I frantically said. "Is Marlene there?"

I didn't want to risk Marlene being there, overhearing our conversation and then hurting Agnes.

"She's not. She went away for a couple days after she dropped me off at the hospital." Agnes said.

"Hospital?" I didn't recall Agnes mentioning to the Divas that she was going to the hospital.

"I just couldn't take it anymore. I went in and had my eyes fixed." She sounded tired, "Marlene is going to be so surprised when she comes back tomorrow night to pick me up at the hospital and they tell her I've gone home early."

"What do you mean?" I asked, trying not to alarm Agnes.

"The doctors said I would be in the hospital for three days. There wasn't anything for Marlene could do for me, so she left a note with the nurse saying she was going to visit friends for a couple days and for me not to worry because she'd be back to pick me up."

I looked at the clock, and then at Donovan. I had twenty-four hours to get all my evidence together before Marlene attempted to show her face again. I was going to be ready for her.

"I called a cab and came home as soon as the doctor said I was healing nicely." There was obvious pride in her voice.

"Agnes, I will be over in the morning to bring you some breakfast." I knew Agnes had opted for one of Jim's security systems and had the monitor put in her house.

At least that's what Jim had told me when he was trying to sell me monitors for my shop. I wanted to get my hands on Agnes' and see if Marlene had been up to anything.

"I'd love the company," she said. "But my eyes still aren't completely healed. The doctor said it could take weeks to get my good vision back."

"Perfect." My plan was coming together. "I will see you in the morning."

I let Donovan in on my conversation and plan.

"While you're doing that, I will see what I can salvage from Sean's message." Donovan pointed to the kitchen table where my old answering machine sat.

"But tonight, you and Willow will sleep in my guest bedroom. There is now way I'm letting you go home with that nut job on the loose out there."

I didn't fight him. It was the best night's sleep I'd had in days.

Chapter Thirty-Four

"Wake up, sleeping beauties." Donovan flicked the light on. "It's nine o'clock."

I was momentarily confused. I'd forgotten where I was. The bed was so comfortable compared to the bed in the furnished cottage.

I wasn't complaining about the cottage because I loved it. I had just forgotten how nice a really good mattress could feel.

"I have a tee and sweats that might fit you." He sat them on the dresser. Before he walked back out, he said, "I really don't want you to go to your house so try to make those fit."

Why in the world did I learn all those defensive moves if I can't use them? I rolled over and looked Willow in the eyes. She nestled her snout against my cheek. Willow enjoyed a good snuggle, and so did I, but there was more investigating to do.

I threw back the covers and changed into the tee shirt and sweats he had left. It was the exact same tee shirt he was wearing when my face planted into his chest. If I recall correctly, I was trying to get away from Bernadine and her questions, only to be completely embarrassed. That shirt would be tattooed in my brain forever.

"Good morning." I got Willow's leash. "Come on, Willow."

I walked her up and down Donovan's street a couple times, giving her ample time to do her business. There were a lot of people who stopped and stared.

What? Have these people never seen a slightly chunky woman walking a pig with a beaded collar attached to a hot pink leash?

But I didn't say anything. I didn't plan to make this a daily walk for us. I'd probably never see these people again.

The freshly brewed coffee smelled heavenly. I couldn't wait to get a cup. I helped myself by getting my own mug and pouring some of the fresh brew.

I pulled a stool up to the counter and watched Donovan take apart my answering machine.

"Unfortunately, the tape looks like it's been cauterized to the roller." He pointed into the machine with a very small screwdriver, showing me what he was talking about.

"Just salvage anything you can." I pleaded, and then took a sip of the coffee.

There might be little hope to save some of the tape, but I wasn't giving up hope yet.

"Why don't you leave Willow here so you can snoop around Agnes' house without worrying about her in the car?" He looked up, and for a brief moment, I thought I saw some real concern on his face. "Be careful and take your ePhone with you."

"How did you know I have an ePhone?" I knew we'd never talked about it and I hadn't told Cheri.

He pulled his ePhone out of his pocket. I had no idea he had one too. He showed me the symbol next to my phone calls that I had placed to him.

"This phone is amazing. It tells you what type of phone people are calling from." He pushed all sorts of buttons.

I had no clue what he was doing. I had to admit, I did need to learn how to use the phone, but that was on the back burner until I got out of this mess.

"Very cool," I said, and then I patted Willow on the head. "I need to get out of here while I have a window of time."

With the way my luck was going, Marlene would show up early and catch me snooping around Agnes' place.

I waved bye to Donovan. "I'll let you know what I find out," I yelled over my shoulder before I slammed the front door.

I had told Agnes I'd pick up breakfast for us. I hoped she liked White Castle breakfast sandwiches, because I needed a coffee. Besides, who doesn't like White Castle?

With my coffee and sack of breakfast sliders, I was off to Agnes'.

There wasn't a time I could remember being so excited to go to Agnes' house. I just knew there was going to be another big break in the case today. There had to be. The deadline Noah Druck had given me was quickly approaching.

I pulled up to the curb a few houses down the street from Agnes' house. I didn't want to make it obvious that I was visiting Agnes.

Before I got out of my car, I called Donovan.

He answered immediately. "What's wrong?"

"Nothing," I said to put him at ease, although I thought it was cute that he was worried. "I just wanted to let you know that I was here."

"Any luck on my answering machine?" I held out a glimmer of hope with my fingers crossed.

"I did get the tape freed from the roller. I'm in the process of trying to piece it together." He paused. "I'm afraid there's going to be a good portion that I won't be able to save."

I smacked the stirring wheel. That wasn't what I wanted to hear.

"At least something is better than nothing." I tried to sound positive. "I'll keep you posted about what I find here."

I grabbed the White Castle bag and walked up to Agnes' house. I was glad that no one was walking or driving by. Not that it would be unusual for me to be visiting Agnes. She was a divorced Diva, after all. The community was used to seeing us together, but the fewer people that noticed me, the better. Noah didn't need to find out that I'm doing my own snooping around. He'd hear everything I had to say soon enough.

Chapter Thirty-Five

I tapped on Agnes' screen door and even pulled on it, but it was locked. The main door was also locked, which struck me as odd. Agnes always kept that door open unless it was during the winter or at night, and it was neither.

I knocked louder and looked into the lead glass window next to the door, but there was no movement. No silhouette of a floating feather attached to Agnes' turban.

I got an uneasy, almost queasy feeling in the pit of my stomach. Something wasn't right. I jogged around the back of Agnes' house and through her beautiful garden, quickly checking the gardeners' shed. I wanted to make sure she wasn't in there. Agnes took pride in her yard and was constantly working on it.

That door was also locked. I turned and trotted to the back door.

"Whoa!" I grabbed my ankle as I fell to the ground.

I looked into the hole I stepped into, but there was nothing in it, just freshly dug dirt. Agnes was always moving bushes and plants around her yard.

I got up and brushed myself off. There was no way I was going to let a little twist of an ankle keep me down.

One step at a time, I stepped up onto the back porch and peeked in the door, trying to look through the eyelet curtains. The only thing I could see was sunlight shining through a cracked window.

Cracked window!

Without thinking, I dragged a porch chair under the cracked kitchen window, slid the glass up and hoisted myself through it.

Once inside, I parted the curtains and looked outside to make sure no one had seen me crawling through. Spending any time in jail for murder or breaking and entering was not in my future plans.

I thought Agnes must have had a doctor's appointment and forgot about it. She'd probably called my house to cancel our meeting.

That might be a good thing. I wouldn't have to sneak around to find the video monitors if she was out of the house. I slid the window closed. There was no way I was leaving the same way I'd come in.

I walked through the kitchen and fell to the ground when I saw a tiny red light shining in the corner of the wall near the ceiling. Her security camera was pointed right at me or the spot I'd been standing.

Since Agnes wasn't home, I didn't want anyone else to know that I was here. If I showed up on the security video, I would definitely go to jail, but the only place to roll out of sight was under the high-back antique couch.

There was no way I was rolling my whole body under there. Until I considered going to jail.

"One, two,three," I whispered and then closed my eyes.

It took two complete rolls to make it completely into *The Under*. I crossed my arms over my chest and took three deep breaths. *Be aware of your surroundings*, I repeated over and over in my head until my eyes popped open and my adrenaline took over.

I plotted my strategy. I could roll behind the couch and crawl along the wall out of view of the camera.

I thought about the layout of Agnes' house and I remembered exactly where her bedroom was. I guessed that the monitors were in there.

"One, two,three." I closed my eyes again and rolled out. I ended up behind the couch.

That wasn't so bad. Still, I was never going to do *that* again.

Agnes' bedroom door was slightly cracked open. I nudged it with my head while I was still in a four-point crawl stance. My knees ached and were killing me. I felt a little like Willow, hoofing it around the house.

When I got inside Agnes' bedroom, I pushed the door closed with my foot. It was pitch black, completely dark. I ran my hand up the door casing, feeling around the wall for the light switch and flipped it on.

"Eeck!" I screamed, and then fell back to the floor when I saw someone flailing around on Agnes' bed.

The bed moved and squeaked across the hardwood with each thrust of whoever was in the bed.

I got to my knees and slowly extended my body to look over the footboard.

"Agnes?" I jumped to my feet when I noticed poor old Agnes Pearl hog-tied to her own bed and gagged with her purple turban.

The red feather was fluttering out of her mouth like she was a cat that just ate a bird. Her eyes were as big as saucers.

"Who did this to you?" I asked, gingerly removing the turban from her mouth.

Her tongue was hanging out as she gasped for air. I quickly untied each of her limbs, and grabbed a bottle of water that I found on her nightstand.

Once she calmed down, she began to speak.

"I don't know," she sobbed.

In all the years I'd known her, I had never seen Agnes Pearl cry. I've seen her curse a man and yell, but never cry.

"My eyes aren't too good yet, but in the middle of the night, I heard my door open." She took the turban and wiped at the tears that were streaming down her cheeks. "I turned on my bedside light and there they stood. Before I could get a word out, they had me bound, gagged, and tied like a pig. No offense to Willow."

"None taken." I rubbed her arms, trying to give her some comfort.

I was just glad that I'd broken in and found her.

"Did they say anything?" I tried to jog her memory, but she was too upset to talk about it.

She shook her head. "The only thing that got me through it was knowing you were coming over this morning." She reached for the rotary phone next to her bed.

"What are you doing?" I asked, starting to hand it to her.

"I'm calling Noah Druck," she stated.

"Wait." I pulled the phone back to my chest, out of her reach.

This could be the final clue to complete the mounting evidence I already have against Marlene.

"Wait? Are you out of your mind, Holly Harper?" Agnes was back to her spry old self. "I've been lying here, scared out of my mind and waiting for you to find me, and you want me to wait longer? No, no, I'm not waiting any longer."

There had to be footage on the security video of someone walking around, unless they had crawled to reach their destination like I had. That wouldn't be Marlene's style. There was no way she was going to take the chance of breaking a nail. I bet she'd already had the one replaced that I found under my futon.

"Agnes, I really do think Marlene is the one who killed Doug." I sat at the edge of the bed with the phone tight against my chest. "I think she's done something with Sean. I have a lot of evidence I need to get together and then take to Noah."

Agnes Pearl propelled herself out of bed like she had a spring under her. "I want her found and arrested *now*!"

She took the turban and pulled it back over her thinning hair, over her ears, and then tucked in the unruly whispies. Not even a good hog-tying could keep her down.

She grabbed the phone from me. "I'm calling Noah." Her arthritis-ridden index finger punched in the numbers.

"Where are your video monitors that Jim put in?" I asked, while she dialed Noah.

She shook her head, the feather slapping her face each time. "Noah, it's Agnes Pearl, you need to come to my house as soon as you get this message." She slammed the receiver down, got up, and motioned for me to follow her with the old phone still tucked under her arm.

"Agnes, put the phone down." I reminded her she still had it.

She reached behind her and grabbed the phone cord that plugged into the wall. In one swift yank, the cord unraveled to a crazy length.

"Goes with me everywhere." She patted the old thing. "That is one thing that Doug Sloan did do that was right. Got me a long phone extension. Noah should be calling any minute."

I wasn't going to fight with Agnes Pearl. If she didn't want to let go of the phone, she didn't have to.

"Ouch." Agnes smacked into the doorframe. She rubbed her arms and continued walking into the other room. "That damn doctor said this blurriness would go away, and I can't wait."

"Focus, Agnes." There really was no time to spare. We had to see what was on that video. "Where are the. . ."

"Monitors---right." Agnes turned and walked out the door and right into the family room wall. "In there." She pointed the hand that was holding the phone toward the kitchen and rubbed her forehead with her free hand. "In the pantry."

The pantry? That didn't make much sense, but most things in Agnes' world often didn't make sense.

"Okay." I grabbed Agnes by the arms and helped her over to her easy chair. "Sit here. I'll be right back."

I wasn't a doctor, but it seemed to me that Agnes' eyes were worse now than they'd been before. I wasn't about to say anything. I made sure she was safe and then headed to the kitchen.

Voila! Like a shiny new bicycle, the monitor was mounted on the pantry wall off the kitchen. It looks like she'd tried to disguise it with empty cereal boxes.

There were four split frames that showed the family room, garden, foyer and the front yard. Quickly, I dialed Donovan. This was all a confusing mess to me.

Donovan answered the phone on the first ring. "Did you get the information you need?"

"Slight change in plans, but I'm not sure how to get the video footage off Agnes' monitors. It's completely different than the VHS tapes." I briefly described how someone had tied Agnes up and I told him I wanted to see if it was Marlene who had done it. If she had, I'd have more evidence against her and be able to prove my innocence, and hopefully find Sean.

"Who are you talking too?" Agnes screamed from the other room.

Ignoring her, I described the equipment, and Donovan said it was likely streaming footage to a memory card or a computer server.

Donovan asked, "Why would they tie Agnes up?"

I hadn't thought of that. It was a great question and I didn't have an answer for it. I ran back into the family room, feeling a little like Flora with my ePhone stuck to my ear.

"Agnes, where is Marlene's big yellow diamond?" I looked up at the mantel where I remembered seeing it last. I didn't see it, so I patted my hand along the top of the mantel in case it was lying up there. All I came up with was dust on my fingertips.

"Who are you talking to?" She asked, and then began to yell, "Help! Noah, help!"

"It's not Noah." I ran back to the pantry.

"Holly, what is going on?" Donovan sounded very confused.

"Nothing, I'm just trying to figure this monitor out." I had to take care of one thing at a time. Getting the video footage of whoever did this to Agnes was the most important issue at that moment.

The Spinel was gone, along with Marlene. I wondered if Agnes found out the truth about the Spinel and had questioned Marlene about it. Marlene might have flown off the handle.

"What's wrong with Agnes' cat?" He asked.

"Cat?" As far as I knew, Agnes didn't have any pets. "I don't think she has a cat."

"What is that noise in the background? It sounds like a sick cat."

I pulled the phone away from my ear and listened for the noise he was talking about.

"Hooooolly!" Agnes' screamed. "Who are you talking too?"

Damn! It was Agnes that he was hearing.

"Oh, that old cat is Agnes screaming for me." I shut the pantry door behind me, trying to drown her out.

Donovan told me how to retrieve the footage before we hung up. I went back into the family room to try to reason with her one last time.

"Listen," I said, and bent down next to her. "I have to go to my cottage and get the rest of the evidence I've been collecting, or else Sean might not live to see the end of this thing. Marlene kidnapped him, and there is a good chance he could be dead. But I'm hanging onto the small chance that he might still be alive."

That was a thought I had to keep in my head. I've spent a lot of time dreaming and plotting with the Divas about Sean's demise, but it had just been harmless daydreaming that I never thought would come true.

Agnes eased herself up and stood face to face with me. "I'll get my purse."

315 Strung Out To Die

"What? What purse?" I was confused. "Do you think your purse is missing? Is anything else missing?"

I looked around, but nothing seemed to be out of order or even turned over, as you would expect in a robbery. The only things missing were Marlene and her diamond.

"There is no way you're leaving me here." She crossed her arms. "I'm coming with you."

"You need to stay here and wait for Noah." I guided her back into her chair. There was no way I was going to take her out of the house in her current outfit of rainbow bright tights, lime green long-sleeve shirt and purple turban.

"One last question before I go," I said as I slowly turned around to face her again. "What did they take? Is anything missing?"

I found it hard to believe that Marlene would want to tie up Agnes like that. Even if she were behind the murder, she would know that she'd be a suspect. Agnes had offered Marlene room and board, along with everything she could possibly need and more. Agnes even paid Marlene to help her, but in reality, it was for companionship. All the Divas knew the truth.

"That's what I keep asking myself," she answered with sadness in her tired eyes. "You know she buried that damn diamond."

"She did? Why?" I asked.

There had to be more to the story about the diamond than Mimi and Tallulah had told me. I wondered if Marlene had poisoned her ex-lover.

"The day you came by, she was in the back digging a hole, and that is where she buried it," Agnes told me. "If the story she told me was true, I told her to go the police."

"What do you mean, *If* her story was true?" I asked.

"She was very vague when I asked her about her lover and the diamond. She told me that he gave her the spinel and his greedy ex-wife wanted it. She really believes it's hers. I told her it belongs to his family." Agnes' eyes narrowed, a dark shadow cast on her checks from her eyelashes. "She got mad at me for saying that and she stomped out the door."

That would be enough to make Marlene take the diamond and run, but it still didn't give her a reason to tie Agnes up. If Marlene was really a cold-blooded killer, she would've just killed Agnes.

"I'm going to see if the cameras caught anything."

With Donovan's easy step-by-step directions, I replayed the video of Marlene in her leopard print pants tiptoeing into the front door, through the foyer, grabbing the Spinel off the mantel, and disappearing into Agnes' room. The time stamp was 2:15 a.m.

If Marlene thought Agnes was still recovering at the hospital, why would she sneak in? She was living there, and no one would even think twice at her coming in the middle of the night. And she went straight into Agnes' bedroom like she knew Agnes was there.

I hit rewind and watched closely to see if anything was out of place or unusual.

The only thing that caught my eye was something I thought I'd never see. Marlene was wearing flats. I guess she had too. You could hear her coming a mile away in those heels.

I pulled out the memory stick as Donovan had instructed and walked out the back door.

I wanted to check the hole that I stepped in. If I recalled correctly, it was at the same spot Marlene was standing the day I visited, and I remembered how funny Marlene was acting. Maybe there was some evidence left in the dirt.

A shovel was lying next to the newly dug earth along with a pair of gardening gloves. I bent down, put my hand in the dirt, and raked my fingers through the soil to see if anything would turn up. I couldn't feel or see anything. I wasn't about to waste any more time here. I had to get my evidence from the cottage and take it to Noah.

"Told ya."

"Confuse!" Startled, I jumped around with my fists in the air only to see Agnes standing there. "Agnes! You scared me!"

"I said I was coming with you." She planted her hands on her hips. "Now, let's go."

I shifted my weight onto one foot and leaned over toward Agnes. "I think you should stay here and wait for. . ."

"Marlene to come back and kill me?" Agnes shook her head. "You're crazy if you think I'm going to stay here alone. We can go on over to the police station together."

"I have to stop by the cottage to get the rest of the evidence, and then we will go." My cell rang. I brushed the dirt off my hands and grabbed the phone out of my pocket. It was Donovan. "Ugh. Missed the call."

He was going to have to wait. I had to get this information to Noah.

"What is that?" Agnes tilted her head to one side and inched a little closer. "Holly Harper, is that a cell phone?"

I jammed it back into my pocket. Obviously, her eyes were getting better.

"Are you going to wear that?" I asked, ignoring her question.

"What's wrong with my outfit?" Agnes looked down, confirming her eyes really weren't that much better.

"How long did the doctor say your eyes would take to heal?" I asked and motioned for her to come on.

There was no time to take her in the house and change her clothes. We were in a race against time. We had to get to Noah.

"I'm coming." Agnes yelled from behind me, waving her hands in the air.

Chapter Thirty-Six

I tried calling Bernadine on my way home to tell her to row over to my cottage, but she still wasn't home.

I was going to have her go with me to see Noah, just in case he pulled something funny and put me in jail. I could also tell her about Diva Agnes and have Bernadine take Agnes to the police station.

Jim's truck was parked next to the garage when we got there. Seeing it made me feel so much better. Donovan clearly didn't want me to be here alone, and I didn't call to tell him I was stopping by to get the evidence. But with KooKoo Marlene running around, it was nice knowing that Jim was there.

"Wait right here," I instructed Agnes. There was no time to help her out of the car, and have her following me all over the place. "I'll be right back."

Before I went into the house, I decided to go find Jim to let him know I was home. I wasn't going to clue him in on why I was there, but I didn't want him to find me running and screaming away from Marlene if she did show up. I also didn't want him to be scared off by Agnes and her circus outfit.

I'd never stepped foot in the barn before now. It was very neat and tidy. There was a lot of lumber from the hardware store on rows of shelving stacked up to the ceiling. There were several different lift machines along with what appeared to be extra inventory.

"Whoa!" I swung my arms in circles trying to steady myself.

It didn't work. I landed square on my rump. With my hands, I parted the hay on the floor to see what made me fall. I hit something with my hand, and it went rolling into a crease.

"What in the world?" I ran my finger along the crease and stopped when I felt a hinge.

There were actually two hinges that looked like they were attached to a door. *A secret door?*

I lifted up the door and whatever made me fall bounced down some steps. I watched it bounce down each step, revealing itself when it rolled to a stop.

A black and white cat eye bead?

I gasped and clapped my hand over my mouth. I looked around for Jim, but he was nowhere to be found.

For a brief moment, and I do mean brief, I thought about going down those steps, but that was the mother of all <u>Unders</u>.

I couldn't think of anything more *Under* than deep in the ground under a barn.

My head began spinning with many different scenarios. Images of Marlene killing Doug with the cat eyes, kidnapping Sean, tying Agnes up, and now Jim being missing were flashing through my mind.

Marlene was picking us off one by one. I looked back at Agnes, who was waiting patiently like I asked her to and slowly glanced back down into *The Under*.

I felt panicky, but I had to see what was down there. *Be aware of your surroundings*. I took off like a lightning bolt into the ultimate *Under* with my keys firmly planted between my fingers.

It wasn't as scary as I thought it was going to be once I got down there. Jim and Ginger had taken a lot of time making this a very nice barn basement.

I bent down and picked up the cat eye bead and tucked it into my pocket with my ePhone.

There was a nicely lit, tiled hallway leading into a room with Berber carpet, a flat screen TV, and a couple of leather couches. The kitchenette was equipped with a refrigerator, microwave, and sink. Everything someone needed for a snack.

I wondered why after all these years, Ginger had never mentioned this place. Even though she was an honorary Diva, this would have been a great place for the divorced Divas to meet.

I flipped on the TV to see if it worked. There must've been a satellite hooked up to it because we couldn't get cable this far out of the city. I had to remember to ask Jim to tap my cottage TV into it.

It looked like some kind of CSI show, because there were a couple of people bound and gagged on the screen. I went to push the off button when I looked into one of the unlucky guy's eyes.

I grabbed the remote to turn up the volume, but instead I accidently hit another button that changed the channel.

"Oh!" I was shocked to see the inside of The Beaded Dragonfly.

I pushed the button again, and the screen showed the inside of my cottage.

"What the hell?" I whispered, and continued to flip, looking at familiar places, including Agnes Pearl's house.

When I flipped back to the CSI show, I figured out it wasn't a show at all. My face was almost pressed up against the screen looking at Sean, Bernadine, and Marlene, all tied up, unable to move.

Marlene?

I didn't have time to question why Marlene was there. She was the one who was supposed to be doing all the tying up, not being tied. She was the one who I thought was creating havoc on the innocent, not the other way around.

Sean was slumped over, looking tired, almost weak. There were bags around his beautiful green eyes. His shaggy blonde hair was greasy. Even his fake-and-bake tan was beginning to fade.

Marlene had some sort of camouflage pants on instead of her usual skin-tight leggings. The way the camera was angled, I could see she was missing some of her fingernails.

Bernadine's eyes were as dark and angry as a thundercloud. Her light blue silk pajamas had mud stains around the bottom.

I couldn't stand it any longer. This situation was getting more and more complicated---not to mention dangerous. Everything I thought I had figured out was all turning out differently.

I pulled out my ePhone and touched the screen to turn it on. I quickly dialed Noah's number from memory. Surely, he was back at the office by now. Agnes had called him over fifteen minutes ago. I pulled the phone away from my ear and looked at it when I heard it beep. There was a big red 'X' in the upper right corner of the screen.

"No service?" I shook the thing and held it over my head like I'd seen Flora do on several occasions.

I looked at it again. Nothing. Just a big red 'X.'

I had to do something. I didn't have time to try to get the phone to work. There was no time to wait on Noah. This was all in my hands, and I had to find them. I looked back at the TV.

I wasn't scared anymore. I was angry. With my hands held high, I did some defense moves to get warmed up. I didn't know who I was going to use them on, but I would be ready when I did.

"I'm going to find you." I said through gritted teeth, looking at the TV screen as if they could hear me.

Sean looked up at the camera as if he did hear me. There was some hope left in his eyes.

Think, think, think. I tapped my forehead with my finger, hoping this action was going to make me smarter.

I'm just a beader, not a detective or crime fighter. Everything was messed up. Nothing made sense. I was sure I'd had it figured out. Right now was not the time to try to figure it out. I had to get them out of there. But where were they?

I looked at the screen to see if I recognized anything in the room where they were being held. The camera was strategically placed so you could only see the four of them.

"Berber carpet, brown walls." I looked closer. *Berber carpet?* I tapped my foot on the Berber carpet I was standing on. They must be somewhere in this barn.

I ran my hand along the wall for any switches or trap doors like Veronica Mars would have done, but I didn't feel anything. It was just a plain, painted wall.

Thump, thump, thump. There were footsteps coming down the hall. I held my breath. The footprints stopped. I stuck my head around the corner, and in a flash, Marlene, or someone with the same teased out hair, disappeared into a secret passageway off the hallway.

Before the door closed, I tiptoed down the hall and slipped into the passageway just in time. The Marlene look-a-like moved down the long hallway and around a corner.

There were a few doors along each side of the secret passage. I was about to look into one of them when I saw a shadow form on the corner of the wall, coming toward me.

I opened the closest door and shut it behind me. I held my breath until I saw the shadow move past the crack at the bottom of the door. The secret passage door brushed the Berber carpet as it closed.

The light switch on the wall pressed into the side of my arm. I flipped it on. Stacks upon stacks of boxes were all over the padded room. *Padded room?*

I panicked and opened the door. Then I shut it. Where was I going to go? I had no way of knowing where the Marlene look-alike was. She could be outside the door, up in the barn, or in my cottage. Being in here was the safest place to be, for now.

Out of curiosity, I ripped open one of the boxes, and then another, and then another. Box after box was filled with glass beads. One in particular was filled with yarn strands of cat eye beads, just like the ones that I ordered for the shop, and was found around Doug Sloan's neck.

There was no time to waste. I needed to get a hold of Noah. No doubt about it. The big red "X" was still displayed on my ePhone. I snapped pictures of the evidence. I have no idea why, but it seemed like something Veronica would do.

After my impromptu photo shoot, I put my ear back up against the door. It had been a few minutes. I was hoping the coast was clear, because I knew I had to get a hold of Noah and getting out of this barn was the only way to do that.

With my keys gripped tightly in-between my fingers, I slipped out into the hall. A hand gripped my shoulder. As if instinct kicked in, I jumped around, jamming my keys into the attackers gut, bring the attacker to his knees.

"Confuse! Leave!" I yelled, and then I stood over the attacker, ready for another round.

"Stop," he gasped with his hand in the air. "It's me, Donovan."

"Donovan?" I grabbed his hand to help him up. "How did you find me?"

"When I hadn't heard from you, I pinged your ePhone." He stood up and held his stomach. He pulled up his shirt, and in-between the fourth and fifth muscle of his six-pack, there was a deep scratch from my keys.

I really had given him some good jabs.

He held his ePhone up. "I told you that. Your phone can ping other ePhones and see where they are. Kind of cool."

"Thank God, you found me. Did you see anyone in the barn that looked like Marlene?" I asked, grabbing and pulling him into another room when I heard the secret passageway door begin to swing open.

We stood as still at statues until we heard the footprints walk past. Fluorescent lights buzzed and crackled above us when Donovan flipped the switch. This room was much different from the other one. It was empty, with a concrete floor and another door at the far end.

"I didn't see anyone," He whispered into my ear, holding me tight to his chest. "Your car and Jim's truck are parked out there."

"Agnes?" I asked, and pulled away. I walked over to the door and put my ear up to it to see if there was any noise.

"Agnes, what?" He tried to turn the handle, but the door was locked.

I took a stab at it, as if I was stronger than he was, and twisted, pulled and jerked, but it wasn't going to budge.

I stepped back and brushed my hair from my face. "I left Agnes in my car. Did you see her out there?"

"No. I told you I didn't see anyone." He jiggled the handle a couple more times. He looked at me. "What?"

"Agnes insisted on coming with me. I left her in my car." I quickly explained that I was looking for Jim when I stumbled upon The Basement *Under*, what I had seen in the other room with the videos, and how I thought they had to be down here somewhere because of the identical carpet.

"You go check on Agnes. I'll keep looking." Donovan tugged on the door a little harder, giving a good few kicks to the handle. With the third kick, the handle flew off and the door popped open.

We slowly peeked around to see what was on the other side of the door.

"A closet?" There was a bunch of clothes hanging from a rod. "Sean?"

There was no mistaking the crappy overalls Sean wears when he's working. I've always told him that just because he was a handyman, didn't mean he had to dress the part. He wouldn't listen.

"I'd be able to tell these from a million pairs of overalls." I shivered. "We have to find them."

"Go. Call the police." Donovan shooed me out of the room, and out of *The Under*.

I dropped the overalls on the floor on the way out, not looking back.

Chapter Thirty-Seven

The sun stopped me dead in my tracks. My eyes opened and closed trying to focus on my VW. Even with the big sunspot in the center of my eyes, I could tell that Agnes wasn't in the car.

Agnes.

Why couldn't she stay put like I'd asked her?

Stumbling to the cottage, I squinted, trying to see in front of me. I made it to the ornamental concrete pig and stuck my hand in the mouth.

Viola! I took the spare key out of the pig's mouth. I stuck it in the lock and turned. Swiftly, I kicked the bottom corner of the door. It flung open and hit the wall, and then it came back and slammed shut again. Trying to get to the house phone in the heat of the moment, I had forgotten the door had mysteriously become unstuck.

I opened it back up and slipped in, hoping whoever had dressed in Marlene's clothes was nowhere around.

I blinked several times, trying to get my eyes to focus. I had concluded that going in and out of dark places into bright sun and back into the dark couldn't be good for my eyes.

However, I did know my cottage, and with what little sight I did have, I made my way to the landline phone. There was no way I was going to try to focus on my little ePhone.

"I wouldn't do that if I were you," said a voice that came from the hallway.

Frozen, I stopped and looked. The hair was exactly like Marlene's but the damn sunspot was centered right over the face.

"I'm serious, Holly." The voice was loud and bold.

Did they not think I knew that? I had stopped and had not moved.

The hair might match Marlene's, but the voice matched...Jim.

I gulped, blinked, and rubbed my eyes with my fists.

"Jim?" I opened my eyes, and then opened them even wider when I confirmed it was indeed him.

If the situation were different, I would have laughed at seeing Jim in drag.

Eek! I gasped. He was wearing Marlene's clothes and he was wearing flats.

Everything started to come together just like I'd seen in the movies.

, Who would have had access to the shop? Jim. Who owned the building and would be able to get in? Jim. Who would be able to install cameras anywhere in Swanee without anyone questioning him? Jim. After all, Rush Protection Service was his business and the only security business in town.

"Jim?" I asked in utter shock. It was all I could say, "Jim?"

"Shut up, Holly." He walked down the hall, revealing himself in the natural sunlight streaming into the family room. "Aren't you tired of mooching off people?"

What? Mooching? My mouth flew open and then shut. Under normal circumstances, I would have snapped back at him, but these circumstances were anything but normal.

He pulled up Marlene's flowing black chiffon shirt to pull out a gun he had tucked in the waistband of Marlene's leopard print leggings.

"I can see it now." He smiled at his brilliant plan. "You killed Doug because Sean wasn't getting any jobs and was unable to pay your alimony."

I gulped. He was confessing to why he had kidnapped Sean. I listened closely, just in case I did get out of this situation.

I felt my ePhone vibrate in my pocket. *Ugh!* I wished I had taken the extra class the Cell City employee offered. She did say something about emergency calls, and this would definitely be a time for one of those. I couldn't even dial 911 without looking.

Unfortunately, I wasn't feeling too optimistic about getting out of here alive.

"It was so easy to plant everything on Marlene after you started snooping around like that damn pig of yours." He raised the gun up and pointed it at me.

Fear knotted in my gut as I looked down the barrel of the gun.

"Yep, you had to start being the nosey Diva that you are." He threw his back and laughed.

"Jim, you don't have to do this." I said, keeping an eye on the compact weapon.

"Shut! Up!" Jim waved the gun around as if I was confusing him. "It was easy because everyone knows that Marlene wanted Doug for his money. Not to mention the fact that she and Ginger hate each other." He pulled the yellow Spinel out of a pocket on the inside of the leggings. "This was just a little bonus after I installed cameras everywhere and saw Marlene with it."

With his free hand, he flipped the Spinel in the air. The sunlight hit it perfectly and sent sparking prisms all over the cottage walls. After it landed in his palm, he put it back in the little pocket.

"Oh, no." I cried out, and then threw my hand over my mouth.

"Poor Agnes Pearl." He looked at me and his eyes seemed kind of crazed. "She really did think that it was Marlene tying her up."

Agnes? *Think, think, think.* Where in the hell was Agnes? Did Jim see her in my car? Donovan? Oh, how I hoped he wouldn't walk in and get shot by Jim.

"Marlene wasn't too hard to kidnap." Once Jim started talking, he couldn't stop. "I knew Agnes was going in for eye surgery, so I wrote a note so she would think Marlene was going out of town, when all along, I had taken her to my secret spot."

Secret spot? I wondered if Donovan had any luck finding them.

"Sean was the tricky one. I give him credit for fighting, but one knock on the noggin with this," he tapped the butt of the gun, "and he was out."

"Selling his truck was a good idea." Not that I was agreeing with him, but if I did, maybe he'd come to his senses and let me go.

"I was proud of that move." An evil smile crossed his face, and his eyes lit up, making him look like a devil. He lowered his gun and walked around me.

Please don't shoot. I shivered at the thought.

"Oh, and the fudge." He licked his fingers. "You know, Agnes Pearl gave me some of her fresh fudge right before I was going to the Swanee Morgue to install some cameras. Poor Doug was still waiting for the coroner to do his examination. A little fudge under Doug's nails was enough for Noah to suspect Marlene."

He had thought of everything. "Ginger?" I gasped, wondering what he had done to her.

"My baby is fine." He twirled his wedding band with the hand that was holding the gun.

I ducked a few times, fearing he would accidentally shoot and I was in the way.

"Ginger will be sad to see that all her friends have been shot by Marlene." He made a frown. "Including you and the nosiest Diva of all."

"Bernadine?" I had momentarily forgotten about her being tied up in the secret spot.

"She came running over here this morning when she saw me in the wig. She thought I was Marlene and demanded to know why she would be here." He danced on his tiptoes acting like a woman.

Bernadine was only trying to protect me. No wonder she was in her pajamas. My legs felt weak. I couldn't tell if it was from exercising or sheer fright.

"Go ahead." He nodded to the futon. "Sit down."

I eased myself into it without taking my eyes off him. He walked backwards into the kitchen and felt around on top of the refrigerator. He grabbed the baggy with my evidence. "You won't be needing this."

He pointed to the corner of the cabinet, and pulled something off it. "Great little cameras." He held a tiny silver ball in his palm for me to see.

He had been spying on me right along with the rest of Swanee.

"I planted the fake nail when I put Sean's phone in the futon just so you or the police would find it." He laughed even harder, then walked back into the kitchen and looked out over the lake. "I just had to wait in the barn and call his phone with a prepaid cell phone. Generic, cheap, and it worked like a charm."

My throat tightened and my stomach hurt. This was my opportunity. If I was going to get out of here alive, I had to take advantage of it. I knew the door wouldn't stick, so it would make it easier for me to get away, but where would I go?

I was terrified, but I jumped to my feet and without looking back, I ran out the door.

Thump, thump, thump! Jim wasn't too graceful or fast in his flats.

"You better get back here!" Jim screamed, running behind me.

"Confuse and leave!" I screamed, retrieving my keys from my pocket. As if nature took over, like Donovan said it would, I turned and jabbed Jim in the gut.

The gun flew out of his hand and under a bush.
The Under. Damn. The Under.

I plunged my hand in *The Under* and couldn't find the gun.

Jim bolted toward me. I jumped to my feet and grabbed both his wrists before he could get a hold of me. I flung him onto the ground with my knee buried deep into his back. He wrestled around like a bucking bronco, flinging me off and onto the gravel driveway.

"You had better back up." Agnes Pearl was glaring and she had the gun aimed directly at him. Her hands were shaky and unsteady, but I didn't care. Agnes was in control. She blinked a few times. A big smile crossed her face. "Damn, that doctor did a fine job. I can see better now than I have in years."

She extended her arms, and the shaking stopped once she looked down the sight of the gun that she was pointing directly at Jim's heart.

"Jim Rush, you better not move. I'm crazy enough to shoot every limb you got, and make you crawl to your death." Agnes' eyes narrowed.

I had no idea what she was going to do, but I didn't have to worry after I saw a Swanee police cruiser pull into the driveway.

"Help us!" I yelled when I saw Gilley get out of the car.

Immediately, Gilley drew his gun and yelled, "Police! Drop the gun."

Jim started to walk backward with his hands up toward Gilley.

"Don't you move!" I screamed, pointing to Jim. "Gilley, arrest him! He killed Doug Sloan."

"Don't listen to her. I have the evidence to prove that Holly did it and I think she killed or kidnapped the others," Jim said.

"Put the gun down." Gilley was being all calm, cool, and collected, when he needed to be freaking...shooting...Jim.

"Agnes, don't you dare put that gun down." I ordered her to keep her eye on Jim. "Gilley, that's Jim's gun. He had me at gunpoint and Agnes Pearl turned it on him."

"Come on, Mrs. Pearl. We can talk this out." Gilley had his gun focused on Agnes.

"It's Ms., not Mrs. I'm a Diva. A divorced Diva!" Agnes yelled loud and proud.

I wasn't sure, but I'd bet money that Agnes would've taken Gilley down too if it weren't for the sound of a siren approaching in the distance. As it grew louder, I became more confident. I wanted to look toward the barn to see if Donovan was anywhere to be found, but I didn't want to take my eyes off Jim.

Amid flashing lights and a lot of noise, a fire engine and ambulance slid into the cottage driveway, sending gravel flying.

Noah jumped out of the squad car.

"Gilley, put your gun away." Noah ordered as he pointed his gun between us. "Agnes, drop the gun so no one gets hurt."

Agnes dropped the gun at her feet, and stood with her hands in the air.

I was in no situation to laugh, but it was funny to see Agnes Pearl spread eagle in her rainbow bright pants, with her loop-sided purple turban on top of her head. Agnes Pearl might be two cups of crazy, but I guarantee this was the only time that she ever been seen in public *looking* crazy.

"Noah, Holly killed my brother-in-law." Jim pretended to sob. "I have the proof."

All of a sudden, there was a rustle in the woods, a few breaking twigs, and Tallulah and Mimi appeared at the tree line.

"No, she didn't!" Tallulah screamed and ran towards the cottage, waving her finger at Jim. "We heard it all."

Mimi tried to keep up with Tallulah while nodding her head. She followed Tallulah's lead and started to point at Jim.

They were out of breath by the time they made it over to Noah, who looked dumbfounded.

"We were in the woods. And we saw him waving a gun at Holly through the window." She pointed to Jim. "And he kidnapped that hot man, Sean, and some woman."

"He said that Holly was nosey." Mimi chimed in. "Me and Tallulah know that Holly isn't nosey."

Mimi was trying to make me feel better. Tallulah rolled her eyes.

"Hush, Mimi." She turned her attention back to Noah. "Anyway, he has my diamond in his leggings."

Oh. My. God. Of course…the clothes!

"He wanted everyone to believe that Marlene killed Doug. Look at his clothes." I turned to Agnes. "Agnes, it was Jim who tied you up. Not Marlene." Agnes had already dropped the gun.

Noah pointed his gun at Jim, staring down the sight. He motioned his head toward Jim. "Gilley, cuff him."

Gilley was more than willing to grab the cuffs off his belt and slap them on Jim's wrists.

Another car pulled into the gravel driveway.

"Holly?" Sadie asked, getting out of the car and walking up. "This is your house?"

"Sadie?" Gilley slammed the back door shut on the cruiser once he'd put Jim in. "What are you doing here?"

"Gilley? Sadie?" I said, wondering how they knew each other, but still reeling from all the excitement.

"Honey, I'm working." Gilley said.

"What are you doing here anyway?" Noah asked Gilley.

Gilley pulled out a pink slip from his coat pocket. "Holly had come by the station to get her police report, but she left before I found it. I wanted to give it to her so she could file her insurance report."

"She did?" Noah's eyes narrowed. Apparently, he had figured out my little trick. "Well, I'm glad you brought it."

The big barn doors swung wide open. Donovan walked out, followed by Sean, Marlene, and Bernadine.

"What the. . ." Noah stopped and stared.

"That no good Jim Rush!" Bernadine screamed, and stared into the back of the cruiser. "You're lucky you're in there! Or I'd kill you with my bare hands!"

Noah grabbed Bernadine to calm her down. Agnes was comforting Marlene. Sean and Donovan began giving their statements to Gilley.

"Agnes, thank you. You saved my life." I hugged her. "Where did you go?"

She pulled away. "I had to pee. And when a girl has got to go, she's got to go, so I went into your cottage. The door was unlocked, so I shut and locked it just in case Marlene showed up. I turned on your bathroom light and I couldn't believe how well my eyes focused. I heard someone come in, and looked out. I thought it was Marlene, so I slipped back into the bathroom until I heard you."

"So you didn't call Noah from the house?" Confused, I looked to Noah for answers. "Who called? Donovan?"

"I don't know. Someone that was out of breath and screaming for help." Noah shrugged his shoulders.

"It was me," Tallulah admitted. "I was going to bust down the back door right before Holly ran out the front."

I grabbed Tallulah and hugged her.

"Don't hug her," Marlene turned her nose in the air and then turned to Noah. "And would you mind getting my leggings off him. They are one-of-a-kind."

Tallulah pushed Marlene aside, getting to Noah. "Not before I get my diamond out of them."

"It's mine!" Marlene jabbed Tallulah with her broken fingernail.

"Don't you touch my sister." Mimi pushed Marlene out of the way.

"No one is going to touch anyone." Noah stepped between them with his arms spread wide. "We can all take this down to the station."

Everyone was still too scared to say a word. We all piled into our cars and followed Noah back to the Swanee Police Station.

Chapter Thirty-Eight

When we got to the station, Noah put Jim in a holding cell and had us sit on the benches that lined the wall. One-by-one, he questioned each of us regarding our involvement and what we knew.

"How did you come to be involved?" Noah asked Donovan.

"I'm dating Holly and I had a pretty good idea what was going on when I fixed the tape from her answering machine. I found a message that Sean had left her, saying that he didn't think Marlene killed Doug. Up to that point, we thought Marlene was the killer," Donovan said. It was great that he got it fixed, but it didn't matter now.

"What?" Sean and Marlene said in unison.

"Me?" Marlene pointed to her chest. "I wouldn't hurt a fly."

"Dating?" Sean said in a whiney voice and ran his fingers through his hair. "Dating, really?"

I had to put a stop to all this nonsense. It had been a long day and I was ready to finally get some sleep, since the murderer was behind bars.

"Here's how it happened. Doug thought he was meeting Marlene at the bead shop when Jim told him to go there. Jim had a key to the shop because they own the building. He waited for Doug to come into the shop and then strangled him." I took a deep breath, and continued. "He was going to blame Sean, but when I started snooping around and found out Sean didn't do it, he decided to frame Marlene by planting all sorts of evidence to make it look like she was guilty."

Noah was scribbling as fast as he could in his little notebook.

He held the baggie in the air, confirming that the Spinel was safe and that he would figure out who the rightful owner was later.

"Bernadine had told me that she'd seen Marlene come and go from my cottage, but it was Jim dressed as Marlene." I finished the story about how Jim built *The Under* in the barn and showed him the pictures I'd taken with my ePhone.

"You got an ePhone?" Marlene and Sean said. They both were surprised.

"Holly Harper, I don't think I know you anymore. Boyfriend? ePhone?" He asked.

If I didn't know better, I'd say Sean was a little jealous that I wasn't falling all over him for not being dead.

"Anyway, Donovan found them in *The Under*, and that brings us up to now." I sighed with relief that this was all coming to an end.

Donovan leaned over and told me, "There was a trap door in that closet."

"You would've been so proud of me." I smiled and looked in his eyes. "I used the 'confuse and leave' with the key jab on Jim. It worked like a charm."

"I'm proud of you." Sean interrupted.

Donovan shot him a look.

Just about that time, Ginger rushed into the station. I stood up, waiting to see her reaction. With tears in her eyes, she grabbed me and sobbed.

"I guess I'm not an honorary Diva anymore," Ginger said, letting us know that she was not going to stay married to Jim. "I can't believe he installed all those cameras just to spy on people."

I filled Noah in on all the places around town Jim had installed cameras to spy on people and told him about Agnes Pearl. "You can find the control room in *The Under* in the barn."

"*The Under* in the barn?" Ginger asked.

Obviously, she didn't know about *The Under* in her barn, and right now wasn't the time to fill her in.

"Where do you come in?" Noah looked at Sadie.

"I'm Gilley's wife and a Diva." She stated proudly.

"A Diva?" Marlene, Bernadine, and Ginger asked.

"Well, sort of. Holly has been helping me spy on Gilley." Sadie fiddled with her fingers. "Well, I thought he was cheating on me, but evidentially he's just been working a lot of overtime since you were trying to get this murder solved."

I couldn't believe that Gilley was the one I was looking for that night at The Livin' End. When I went in to pee, I had seen him and Noah at the bar asking questions about Sean and Doug.

"But in your picture, Gilley had a. . .um. . .purple Mohawk." I put my hand over my mouth to cover my smile, but I guffawed at the image. There was no resemblance at all.

"It was a few years ago when he had more hair." She laughed. "I'm so sorry, honey."

Gilley obviously had forgiven her. He gathered her up into his arms and gave her a big kiss.

"I'd still love to be a Diva," she said over Gilley's shoulder.

"Oh, no you won't." Gilley shook his head. "How did you find out about the Divorced Divas?"

"I overheard you talking about them with Noah at the house one night." She looked over his shoulder and winked at me.

"I'll call you," I mouthed. Even though she was still married, she'd be a fine addition.

"I've missed a lot." Ginger sat down beside me. Her shoulders slumped and she looked defeated.

"Nothing I can't fill you in on later." I put my arm around her. My friend was going to need a strong shoulder to lean on.

Chapter Thirty-Nine

"What are those?" Ginger pointed to the black velvet pouches lined up on the counter.

"Those, my dear friend, are the sixteen sets of bridesmaid accessories I made for Margaret McGee's wedding." I opened one of the pouches to show her the contents.

I beamed. That feeling of joy and elation that I always dreamed of was there. And it felt good. "My first client."

"Oh, Holly!" Ginger gasped. "Margaret is going to be the prettiest bride in Swanee."

"Two of her bridesmaids are coming in for consults for their weddings next week." A sob of relief broke from my lips "This was exactly what I needed to get The Beaded Dragonfly off the ground."

The door flung open. Agnes was swatting Marlene's hand away, Flora was behind them on her phone, and Bernadine was walking behind Flora, picking the lint off Flora's coat.

I hurried to the storage room to get everyone's projects. Although it had only been a week since Jim Rush confessed to murdering Doug Sloan over the Sloan family fortune, all the Divas were back to their old form.

"You need some help?" Cheri asked when she entered the storage room with Willow by her side.

I nodded and counted out seven bead boards.

"Seven?" Her brow furrowed with curiosity.

"Yes, Sadie May is the new honorary Diva since Ginger has upgraded her status," I said and walked out to greet the group.

"Good." Cheri walked behind me. "Someone closer to my age."

"Hey!" Agnes yelled out and adjusted her purple turban. "I'm feeling pretty young with my improved eyesight."

I set everyone's board out in front of them.

"What in the hell are these?" Agnes picked up the shoelace with all the wooden beads tied on. "I said I was feeling young, but I'm not a child."

Everyone bit their lips. We weren't about to let Agnes in on the secret that it was her project.

"Let me go get some real beads for you." I took the shoelace out of her hands.

"You look great, Holly." Flora took my hand and had me twirl around. "And that's a new outfit."

Over the past week, I'd been walking more and I'd given Food Watchers one more try. This time, I sat with my mouth shut.

"I have lost a little weight." I posed with my hands resting on my hips.

I wasn't use to flirty skirts, but since none of my clothes fit, I had to go to the mall and get some new things.

Ring, ring, ring. Beep, beep, beep. The shop phone and my cell phone both began to ring at the same time.

"Marlene, grab the phone." I threw the shop cordless at her.

"Hello?" I said, answering my cell.

"Hi." Donovan's words flowed out of my ePhone. "How about some take-out and a real DVD movie tonight?"

Marlene interrupted, "Holly, Sean's on the phone." She held it out.

I paused. At that moment, it occurred to me that Sean and Donovan had both been calling non-stop all week long.

"I'm hanging out with the Divas tonight." I was beginning to like this dating gig. "But I can tomorrow night."

"Great," Donovan said. "I'm looking forward to it."

Marlene covered the receiver end of the cordless, and whispered, "You are one naughty Diva."

I grabbed the phone.

"Hello?" I politely, but playfully answered the phone.

"Hey, Hol." Sean was back to using the nickname that he started calling me in high school. "I was wondering if I could come over tomorrow night with some take-out and install the chandelier for you?"

It was the first mention of the heirloom since I'd told him earlier in the week that I had taken it once I realized he was in trouble. I knew he wouldn't leave town without it. I was keeping it for payment for saving his butt.

"Tomorrow?" I looked up at the chandelier hanging from the center of the shop ceiling.

There wasn't anything the Divorced Divas couldn't do.

"I'm busy tomorrow night, but I can the next night." I looked down at my lovely manicured nails that Marlene had painted for me earlier in the week.

After I hung up, I turned around and all the Divas stared at me, shaking their heads.

"Holly Harper, what has gotten into you?" Ginger smiled.

"What?" I shrugged and looked over Flora's shoulders at her chandelier earrings to make sure she was finishing them correctly.

"First, you join the defense class. Then, you join Food Watchers," Agnes Pearl chimed in.

Cheri interrupted, "And, you started walking and lost more weight."

I picked up her stretchy bracelet and put it on her wrist to make sure it fit.

"Don't forget about the new ePhone." Bernadine was still no further along on her project. She had redone the pattern yet again.

"Oh, that." I waved my hands in the air, trying to play it off.

Everything was coming together. The Beaded Dragonfly was finally taking off and the Divas were back.

And better than ever.

Holly Harper's Advanced Beading Class Project: Miss U Heart Swarovski Drop Earrings:

(Designer Jude, Jewelry Production Specialist, Marketing Content Development Group, Exclusively for Fire Mountain Gems and Beads®)

Materials Needed

Bead, Swarovski crystal, crystal golden shadow, 4mm Xilion bicone (6 beads)

Drop, Swarovski crystal, crystal golden shadow, 18x17mm Miss U Heart pendant (2 drops)

Jumpring, gold-plated, 4mm round, 20 gauge (2 jumprings)

Earwire, gold-plated brass, 16.5mm kidney with 4.5mm half-ball with open loop, 21 gauge (2 earwires)

Wire, Wrapit, jeweler's bronze, dead soft, 20 gauge

Pliers, nylon jaw

Pliers, flush-cutter

Pliers, round-nose

Pliers, chain-nose

Pliers, bent-nose

Pliers, flat-nose

STEP 1

Cut a 5-1/2 inch length of jeweler's wire. Form a 5-loop flat spiral on one end of the wire.

STEP 2

Bend the straight end of the wire so it passes through the center of one 17mm Swarovski Miss U Heart drop and back through the center of the flat wire spiral.

STEP 3

String onto the straight end of the wire three 4mm Swarovski bicone beads. Form a simple loop on the straight end of the wire.

STEP 4

Open a 4mm round gold-plated jumpring and pass it through the simple loop formed in Step 3 and the loop on a gold-plated kidney earwire. Close the jumpring.

Repeat Steps 1-4 to create the second earring.

A Note From The Author

Thank you so much for reading my novel. I'm truly grateful for the time we have spent together. Reviews are very important to an author's career and I would appreciate it if you could take a couple minutes of your time by clicking on the click below and leaving a review for my novel. Thank you so much, and I hope we continue to meet in the world of books. ~Tonya Kappes

About The Author

International bestselling author Tonya Kappes spends her day lost in the world of her quirky characters that get into even quirkier situations.

When she isn't writing, she's busy being the princess, queen and jester of her domain which includes her BFF husband, her teenage guys, two dogs, and one lazy Kitty.

Tonya has an amazing STREET TEAM where she connects with her fans on a daily basis. If you are interested in becoming a Tonya Kappes Street Team member, be sure to message her on Facebook.

For more information, check out Tonya's website, www.Tonyakappes.com, for all the latest news and events

17015204R00211

Made in the USA
Charleston, SC
22 January 2013